MW01592554

WRITERS REPUBLIC

MIRROR IMAGE

YOU CAN NOT AIRBRUSH A SELF-PORTRAIT

MJ WATSON

WRITERS REPUBLIC L.L.C.
515 Summit Ave. Unit R1
Union City, NJ 07087, USA

Website: *www.writersrepublic.com*
Hotline: *1-877-656-6838*
Email: *info@writersrepublic.com*

Ordering Information:
Quantity sales. Special discounts are available on quantity purchases by corporations, associations, and others. For details, contact the publisher at the address above.

Library of Congress Control Number: 2022902227
ISBN-13:   979-8-88536-003-6   [Paperback Edition]
                  979-8-88536-004-3   [Digital Edition]

Rev. date: 05/09/2022

Fall 1995

Chapter One

"Hi Gram"

"Hello Claire, good morning. Did I get you out of bed?" I ask as Claire answers the door and sees me, her grandmother here with a gift wrapped in birthday paper.

"No Gram, come on in. I've been up just a little while though. I see you brought Greg's birthday present."

"Yes I did, I'm on my way into Portland to look for a dress to wear to Steve Martelli's wedding in a few weeks. Since Grandpa died I haven't felt much like doing anything. This is the first doings I am going to without him."

"Oh, come on Gram, don't feel bad, I think it is a great idea to buy a new dress, you deserve to look beautiful, I sure think so. Besides shopping always makes me feel better."

"Claire, are you the only one home?"

"Yes, my Mom and Dad went to Greg's soccer game. I don't expect them back for at least an hour. Do you want to come in and wait?"

"No, I will leave his gift. I want to find a dress today."

"Okay Gram."

"Claire, come with me, help me find a beautiful dress to wear."

"No, thanks anyway Gram, I'm not even dressed."

"I'll wait for you Claire come on, we'll have fun and lunch. I will take you out to lunch."

"I don't think so, I didn't sleep well last night and maybe I will lie down for a little while."

"Claire, you're going to be tired tonight whether you nap today or not, so go get dressed quick and come with me."

"Gram, I really don't feel much like shopping."

"Claire, you just told me shopping always makes you feel better. Plus we're going to have a nice lunch. You go get ready and I will write a note to your parents telling them you are with me and we went shopping."

"Okay Gram, you talked me into it, I'll be quick. There is note paper next to the kitchen phone."

I'll leave a note wishing Greg a Happy Birthday and letting them know Claire went with me into town. I am saying all this out loud as I write the note. Waiting I see Claire walking slowly down the stairs and I think she does look awfully tired. I ask her, "You do look tired Claire, were you up late last night?"

"Not really, we watched a movie at Erin Price's house and I was home by eleven. I didn't feel good. I didn't sleep well either."

"Well, what do you say, let's get going Claire?"

"Did you leave a note?" Claire asked.

"Yes, on the kitchen table. I also told them you would call in a few hours so don't forget."

"Great, 'let us be gone', as Dad says."

"Yes 'let us be gone' as your Dad does say."

"Gram, would you mind if I drive to town?"

"Yes, I would mind, I'll do the driving; you ride, and put your seat belt on."

"Oh, yes ma'am."

"Claire did you send your application to the University of Portland and that other school? What's the name of the other school you are considering?"

"I am considering Gonzaga University in Spokane Washington and Pepperdine University in Malibu California."

"Yes, Pepperdine, that's the one, I can never seem to remember the name of that school. Did you apply at all three?"

"No, not yet, Dad wants me to go to Portland or Gonzaga, we get a brake on tuition at those two colleges because he teaches at Portland."

"Annie loved Gonzaga U."

"I know, she wants me to go there."

"Claire all things being equal which school would you choose right now?"

"I don't really know or care. I can't think about that right now Gram."

"Why can't you? You should be getting ready now and sending in your applications so you can make you decision as early as possible."

"Gram, I just can't think about that now, it's not important, I have a lot of time before I have to apply!" Claire replies sharply.

"Claire, I just asked, you don't have to raise your voice to me."

"I know Gram, I'm just not thinking about college right now."

"Claire first we will stop at the mall and find a dress for me to wear then we will go downtown for lunch. How does that sound?"

"That sounds good to me."

———————•— —•———————

"Claire lets put these bags in the trunk so no-one sees them when we park downtown. Are you ready for lunch?"

"Sure Gram, but I really don't feel much like eating."

"Well if you're not hungry yet, let's stop at the drug store, I need to pick up a few things. Claire bringing you along is lucky. I found a dress so quick and I am very happy with the shoes and purse. They will look great with the dress we picked out."

"I agree. You'll look great at the wedding."

"Claire, what's wrong? You said barely a word in those stores and you were rude to the sales lady when she suggested the horrible green dress."

"That dress was gross and she knew it, then you said 'maybe I'll try it on'!"

"Claire, do not snap at me! What's wrong, your mood changed? Why are you upset? Do you want to spend the day with me? Why did you come if you're in such a bad mood?"

"If you remember correctly Gram, I did not want to come."

"Claire, I'll just take you home if it would make you feel better?"

"No Gram, I will go to the drug store with you."

I pull up to a stop light and look over at Claire, she doesn't so much seem sick, as she seems sad. She looks out her window to avoid talking. As I pull away from the light I glance over again and our eyes caught, she

3

is sad, it seems very sad. I ask her as I drive downtown. "Claire what is bothering you? I know it's not just being too tired or not feeling good. There is something heavy on your mind and on your heart."

"Gram, it's nothing, I am fine!"

I pull over and stop the car at the curb, slide the gear into park, and turn my body to the right. As I look at Claire she continues to look forward out the window then Claire turns her head and looks questioningly at me. "What?" she asks.

I don't answer. I am looking right into her face and see a look, familiar, yet, what is it? When have I seen this look before? I brake the silence as I softly and slowly ask, "When is your baby due Claire?"

"Pardon me?"

Again I ask "When is your baby due?"

"Gram do you think I am pregnant?"

I am silent.

"What makes you think I am pregnant?" Claire asks with anger in her voice.

"I am a woman too Claire and that is just what I see."

"Well guess what Gram, I'm not! So let's get going to the drugstore."

I turn my attention back to the car and slowly pull away from the curb and calmly into traffic. We both remain quiet as we continue on to the drugstore. There is a parking spot right in front of O'Brien's drugstore, and I parallel park with ease. "Do you need anything while we are here Claire?"

"No, I'll just look at the magazines while you shop."

"Great, well if you find something you want while I am shopping let me know."

It's not long before I have the things that I need in my cart, when I begin to look for a few greeting cards for some upcoming occasions. None of the cards strike my fancy. I can't concentrate on the cards and I decide to look for cards later. I push my cart toward Claire as she fingers through a magazine and I ask her, "Can I buy that for you?"

"Not this one Gram, but I would like the People Magazine over there."

"Sure, put it in the cart and I'll check out. I'll meet you up front in a few minutes."

"Thanks Gram."

As we walk out of the store I ask Claire. "Where would you like to eat?"

"To tell you the truth I am really not hungry, the thought of eating makes my stomach hurt."

"How about a sandwich, salad, or a cup of soup for lunch, maybe a little something will help you feel better?"

"No Gram, nothing for me, so you decide what you want and that is where we will go. I don't care I am not going to eat. I'll have a coke."

"What about pie, a piece of apple or pumpkin pie? Frankie's coffee house is right across the street, let's go there."

"Alright but no pie for me, I am not hungry."

"How about a piece of cheesecake, maybe you would like a piece of cheesecake?"

"I don't think so. I think I'll have a cup of hot chocolate."

As we enter the coffee shop I suggest that we take a table in the window. There are only two other tables occupied both on the other side of the café.

"Can I get coffee for you ladies today?" Frankie asks.

"Yes for me regular coffee, no flavoring and a piece of pumpkin pie. Claire?"

"I'll just have hot chocolate please."

"Good choices, your order will be right up. Thank you."

"This coffee shop reminds me of a malt shop I went to when I was your age."

"I'm sure!"

"It does, the long counter and stools are just how I remember when I was young. I think that's why I like coming here. All this chrome and mirrors, it brings me back to my high school days." I pause for a moment. "Claire, you still didn't tell me when you're due?"

"Gram, I'm not having a baby! Don't you understand English? What? Was Aunt Marge or Aunt Annie pregnant when they were my age? Just what is it that makes you think I'm pregnant?"

"I know Claire because I have seen it before?"

"What have you seen before?"

"Claire, I have seen a seventeen-year old pregnant woman before. I am not mistaking. There is not doubt in my mind. It is very risky for me to say this to you however I know what I see."

"Who was it Aunt Marge or Aunt Annie?"

"Stop it Clair, it was not them."

"Then who was it?"

"Claire, this is not the end of the world for you. You are old enough to have a baby, to be a mother, to have a child and care for a child."

"Old enough, you think I am old enough? I'm seventeen years old; I'm a senior in high school and have all of college to do."

"You will be able to do all of that."

"Wait a minute, who said I was pregnant? I didn't!"

"I did Claire, remember, I asked you when your baby was due, which you still did not answer."

Frankie approaches the table carrying a tray. "Coffee and pie for you Miss, the cream is here. Your hot chocolate will be just another minute."

"Thank you Frankie, this pie looks good; I will wait until you get your hot chocolate Claire."

"Gram, I don't know where you get your information, but you got this one all wrong."

Frankie returns to the table. "Here we are, hot chocolate for the young lady."

"Thank you."

"Will there be anything else?"

"No, everything is fine, thank you."

Sipping their hot drinks Claire looks up and asks. "Gram, what makes you think I am pregnant?"

"I recognize the signs. You know they are just about the same for all seventeen-year-old expectant mothers."

"They are? What signs?"

"Oh the usual, they are not, 'what dress to wear' or 'will I be accepted at this college' or 'will he ask me to homecoming' signs. They are grown up signs, signs of a woman, not a girl. They are signs of commitment, decision and of maturing, signs of confusion, uncertainty, and anxiousness. You know pompom, fast pitch softball and the prom are somehow no longer important."

"Pompoms never were important, really Gram?"

"Well I was interested in cheerleading when I was in high school, and we had pompoms.

You know Claire having a baby is the most beautiful experience a woman goes through in her life under the right conditions. Loving a man, he loving her, being married helps.

However, a man and woman can conceive a child without love or marriage. Even this does not take away the feeling of mothering, that very natural love, that mother's love will always be there. I can't explain it Claire. Have any of your friends become pregnant?"

"None of my close friends, at least not that I know about."

"What do you mean?"

"Well maybe they wouldn't tell anyone if they decided not to keep the baby."

"Are you talking about adopting the baby out or are you talking about abortion?"

"Well either I guess but I was thinking about abortion. No! No! Not me! I mean I think that is what girls consider today!"

"Girls do consider having the baby and then adopting out? They do, don't they Claire?"

"Probably Gram, I don't know. I think some keep their babies but most end it before anyone finds out. Most girls don't even tell their best friends, not even their boy friend, but sometimes you can tell by the way she acts."

"Exactly, my point exactly, by the way the girl acts! By the way the girl acts! By the way you're acting."

"Gram, please stop, I'm not pregnant."

"So you say."

"Gram, I'm not!"

We are both quiet, looking down at our food. "Claire," I am quit for a moment "the decisions you make today will be with you the rest of your life, like the decision of what college to attend. You want to enter a college that offers a good program in the field you want to study. You don't pick a school because a friend is going there. You might change schools after a year or two and you could likely change majors before you settle on one, but you choose a school that will best suit your different interests, weighing all of this with cost, location and so on."

"I know Gram all three of these schools offer what I am looking for. I would like to go to Pepperdine but it would cost my parents a lot more money."

"Yes, so that too must be considered and put into the decision making. Having a baby at seventeen, not married and very much wanting to go to school presents one with many things to think about, consider and decisions to make. Today society offers and many times encourages a young mother to end her pregnancy, end the problem and abort the baby. Abortion does end the pregnancy, the baby is gone but the problem is not solved. Believe me I know this does not solve the problem. See Claire you're pregnant and sometime in the future you will no longer be pregnant. However the pregnancy ends, through miscarriage, abortion or completion to birth, the fact remains you were once pregnant. We want to believe that having an abortion means everything goes back three or four months, to no pregnancy. It doesn't, you can never go back. After choosing and having an abortion the mother will discover that dealing and living with the embarrassment and shame of being an unwed mother is nothing in comparison to what she will live with knowing she aborted her child. This is true even if she chooses never to tell anyone. Claire the decisions you make today, this week or whenever will affect you the rest of your life."

"Gram, why are you preaching to me about all of this? I told you I am not pregnant! I wish you would just stop."

"Claire, a long time ago I was in the same situation you are in today. Things were very different, I had to leave home during the pregnancy and I too was a senior in high school planning to go to college. It turned out that I was very selfish and aborted my baby. To this day my heart aches for that child, my child I killed. Claire, I can see that you are going through much of the emotional turmoil I went through. Let me help you. Don't make the horrible choice I made."

Claire wipes her eyes with her napkin, as she sets the napkin down, I take both her hands in mine, she is crying, we are both crying. "Gram, I'm scared, I'm so afraid."

"Do your parents know?"

"My mother knows, she thinks having an abortion is the best thing at this point in my life."

"What about your Dad?"

"He doesn't know. You know how he is!"

"How do you feel?"

"Awful, I just want this all to end."

"Claire, this is never going to end. When it is over you can and will look back at the abortion, the life that you ended or the fact that you don't know your own child that someone else is raising. You will wonder everyday what she looks like or does he like sports? It will be hard, unbearable at times. I can with all honesty say I wish my heart ached to know my child, is she married, what kind of work does he do? That pain and horrible for sure has hope. The pain that will never go away from aborting your child is empty of hope. The tears of sorrow will never rinse away the sadness I feel everyday.

Forgiveness, I have received forgiveness, and it is God's forgiveness that allows me to accept what I did. And his graces helped me to move forward."

"Gram, can we go? Please take me home." "Okay, why don't you go to the car, it is across the street while I pay the bill." "Did you enjoy the pumpkin pie?" Frankie asked as I approached the counter to pay.

"It turns out that neither of us is very hungry. But, thank you very much; I'm sure it is good pie."

"Well come back and next time the pumpkin pie will be on the house."

"Thank you."

"Claire, do you want to go home, or perhaps take a ride, or come to my house for a while?"

"No thanks, I just want to go home."

"Claire, just think"

"Please Gram. Please no more talking, Okay?"

Leaving town and taking the country roads home are so pleasant and relaxing, yet I have much to say. How am I going to tell her I made all these mistakes and don't do what I did? Claire is completely quite and just gazes out the window.

"I can't believe you had an abortion Gram!" Claire whispers.

"Yes, I did and I am truly sorry, there is nothing I regret more. I hope and pray Claire, that you're able to tell your daughter or granddaughter that you did not choose abortion. I hope you're able to tell her you chose what was best for her, for your baby, for you."

"Gram, please stop talking about this stuff."

"Claire, you just said you can't believe I had an abortion, are you surprised at me and what I did?"

"Yes, I am surprised."

"Well think more highly of yourself and don't do what I did. Claire, have this baby, your baby, your child. Tell the young man that he too is having a child. Talk to him, talk to your Mom and Dad. Explain to them that carrying through this pregnancy is what you want to do, and what you need to do. It's what is right. Don't do what I did Claire. It leaves a hole in your heart, in your soul, that will never close."

As we drive up to Claire's house we see her father's car in the driveway and the front door to the house is opened. "Gram, my parents are home, please don't come in, if you do my Mom will know we were talking about this."

"Oh, we forgot to call them! I left the note saying you would call them."

"Don't worry, I'll tell them we forgot."

"Claire promise, we will talk again before you do anything. Please talk to your parents, both of them. Promise me, please promise."

"I will, thank you, I'm glad we talked."

Claire leans over and hugs me.

"Thank you."

"Claire, call me, you promised?"

"I will. Bye."

"Bye Claire, I love you."

Claire runs up the steps onto the porch. She turns and waves good bye and steps in the door. "God be with her." I pray as I pull away.

Chapter Two

*********** *GOING HOME* ***********

"Oh my God be with me. Sacred Heart of Jesus, have mercy on us, all of us." I pray as I view the clouds below me from the window seat of this 737. "My dearest Jesus, I spoke with Claire last night and she said she was going to have her baby. Thank you. Help her today when she talks all this over with her parents. Please dear God be with them, please. Also my dear Jesus, please be with me today as I see my family again. Help them to understand, help me to understand. Please Holy Spirit help me to say what I should say, not too much, but what I should say."

"Where to lady?"

"7789 South Wood Street, Chicago, it's on the south side of the city."

"Where do you want to go?"

"South side of the city, 7789 South Wood, do you know where that is?"

"Yes I do, we're on our way."

"Thank you, how long will it take us?"

"We'll be there in about forty five, fifty minutes. Saturday evening, we should move through the city pretty quick." "Oh good" I say as I lean back and gaze out the window.

"God, I hope I am doing the right thing." I pray.

"Ma'am, we have about another mile. Have you ever been here before?"

"Oh, yes I grew up here. I haven't been here, well, let me put it this way I left in 1951."

"Oh lady, that was long before I was born but I'm sure this is not the same neighborhood you left. Are you sure you are going to the right place?"

"Yes, I believe my family still lives here, some of them anyway."

"Ma'am, I think we should be sure before I leave you here." "Oh my I would never recognize this old neighborhood. Everything is so different."

"Yes Ma'am, this is inner city, not like it was when you left. I don't think you're going to the right place. Here we are 7789 Wood."

"Go around the corner to the side entrance."

"This ride cost you 41.50, and I think I should wait. This is not your neighborhood lady." As the cab driver rolls down the window of the cab I see a young black boy about twelve years old closing the gate, he looks up at us as the cab driver asked "Hey kid, who lives here?"

"Mr. Hinelick. Why? I don't think he called a cab, I'll check."

The boy opened the gate and went back in.

"The cab driver turned and said Hinelick or something like that."

"That's right, this is my stop. How much do I owe you?"

'$41.50."

"O.K. here is fifty, wait, sixty, Thank you very much. Keep the change."

"Lady you're sure this is where you want to go?"

"Yes, I'm sure, I'll be alright."

After stepping from the cab I turn and grab my purse and travel bag, I push the door shut and turn toward the opened gate being held by this young boy. "Do you do odd jobs for Martin Hinelick?" I asked the youngster.

"Yes ma'am I do. Mr. Hinelick is right up there."

I looked up and saw an elderly man looking through the screen. "Hello." I said nervously.

"Hello, can I help you?" He asked as he pushed open the door, peering out. "Martin Hinelick?"

"Yes, who's asking?"

"Daddy, is that you"

"What?"

"Daddy, I'm Doris."

"Doris? Is that you Doris?"

"Yes, yes Dad it's me, Doris." I answer as I grab the porch railing and begin to climb the six steps up to the door.

"Doris Hinelick, is that you?"

"Yes Dad, it's me. I'm here, I've come home."

"Oh my God, Doris you're here, you're alive, and you're home. Oh my God, thank you. Thank you my dearest Jesus, thank you Jesus! Doris, come in here, come in here." He calls as he holds open the storm door while standing in the kitchen. A red and gray flannel shirt tucked in his gray trousers held up by navy blue suspenders closes the elderly man with gray hair neatly groomed.

"Oh my God Daddy it's you! I can't believe it's you, I can't believe you're still here, here in this house."

"Come in Doris, come in! Let me see you, let me see you!"

"Oh Daddy, I've missed you, I've missed you so much."

The storm door slams as Doris sets down her suitcase and purse. She turns toward her father who is leaning back against the opened door holding himself up with his left hand on the doorknob. "Daddy, don't just stand there, I want to give you a hug!"

They move toward each other and hug, both holding tight. Shaking, both shaking, Martin turns his head and sweetly kisses Doris on her cheek, tears run slowly down his cheeks. Doris turns her head and with great affection kisses her father, turns back and squeezes him as they hold each other.

"Doris, let me look at you." Martin says as he steps back to view his daughter.

"Doris, I can't believe you're here. You look absolutely wonderful; you bring joy to these tired old eyes." "I'm fat Dad, I don't look that good." Fat, skinny, tall, short, it doesn't matter just seeing you, knowing you are okay, I can't believe it. Dear God, thank you. Doris, I love you, I missed you, and everybody missed you!"

"Dad, sit down, you need to sit down, and you need to stop shaking. Dad please sit down, we'll catch up."

"I will, okay, okay I'm sitting. Doris we all missed you so much, all of us. I wish Mom could be here to see you. Oh how she missed you. She always believed you would come home. She always said 'Doris will come home when she is ready'. She never stopped praying. Never stopped believing you would come home. I'm sorry Doris, Mom died four years ago next May. Oh how happy she would be to see you. Doris, I can't believe you're here. I can't believe you're home. Lord Jesus Christ, thank you. You look wonderful Doris!"

13

Oh, I'm fat but you look terrific Dad."

"Doris! I'm an old man and I look like an old man. A healthy old man, my heart didn't stop when you walked up the porch steps. Oh how good to see you Doris. Doris I never stopped praying, I hoped you would come home."

"Dad, I'm home, I've come home."

"Yes Doris, you're home."

"Dad, please tell me about Mom."

"Oh Doris she never gave up hope either. Mom's gone, four years next May. Oh she's happy now! Oh how she wanted to see you Doris. Oh how good it feels to say your name."

"Was she sick?"

"Mom had cancer. She wasn't sick long, about four months but the last three weeks were very bad. She finally went peacefully in her sleep on May 25th 1992."

"Dad, I'm sorry. I'm so sorry."

"I wish Mom could have talked to you again, nothing did she want more. But Doris I'm so glad you're home. Oh give me another hug." Doris and her Dad hug and hold each other in silence. Four eyes filled with tears. They held tight and did not let go for what seemed to be a long, long hug. Pulling herself away ever so gently Doris asked, "How's Bernie? Tell me about Bernie."

"Bernie was only fourteen when you left. She is going to be so happy to see you. She missed you so much, well they all did and still do. Wait till they see you!"

"Please tell me about each one but start with Bernie and then Jack."

"Bernie is married, Tom Michaels her husband is and optometrist. They live in Oak Lawn and have four grown children, two girls and two boys. They're all married. Bernie has three grandchildren and she is a teacher and works in the Catholic schools. She's been teaching since the kids were in high school. Bernie will never retire. Tom talks about retiring to Arizona in about three years, but truthfully, I don't think Bernie will ever leave this area, all four of her kids are here and of course her grandchildren."

"I miss her Dad, I'm afraid to call her, but I must call her first, before anyone else. Dad, tell me about you and Mom. When did you retire?

Why are you still here in this big old house all alone? You are alone here aren't you?"

"Yes, since Mom died, it was just the two of us for more than fifteen years.

Tom stayed home until he married in 1977 about half a year after I retired. Tom shares the business now with Nick and Frank. Paul was killed when his motorcycle hit the side of a truck in the fall of 1969. He died instantly and Tom still is not over it."

"Paul is dead?"

"Yes it was terrible. I think your mother would have completely cracked, except she was so concerned for Tom. It was as if Tom died too. Twins have that bond, I just never saw with any of the others. Both sets of twins were like that. Nick and Frank are still close. They share the business and are together all the time. You would think they would need to get away from each other, but they don't. After Paul died they took Tom in kind of under their wings and it's special, different than any of the other kids. All three are married and have families, yet they have this very special bond."

"When I left Mom was expecting number ten, a girl or boy?"

"Annie, she was born later that year."

"Annie! How is Annie? I can't wait to meet her."

"Annie, she is just great, wonderful. She is married and has seven children. That is a big family today. She has the most kids. Her husband's name is also Tom, Tom Schwartz. Their oldest is in high school and youngest is just three, all boys."

"How many grandchildren do you have altogether Dad?"

"I have twenty nine grandchildren. How many children do you have Doris?"

"I have four children, two boys and two girls, all grown of course."

"Well with yours that makes thirty three grandchildren for me. Do you have any grandchildren Doris?"

"Ten."

"Wow-that's thirty seven great grandchildren. Are you a great grandmother?"

"No I am not, not yet."

"How many great-great grandchildren do you have Dad?"

"No great-great grandchildren at this time. Doris how old is your oldest grandchild?"

"She is eighteen this month."

"Dad the neighborhood, it's so different now, it's inner-city?"

"It sure is. When we bought this house in 46' it was just beautiful. I remember your Mom saying 'A corner lot in Little Flower Parish and finally enough room for all of us'.

I remember moving out of the three flat, third floor. Five kids and a new baby, Joey was just six weeks old when we moved here. This has been a good place to live. Almost every white person was gone from this area by the mid seventies. It seemed sad at first all our friends were asking us why we were staying here. When the neighborhood was changing there was a lot of hatred and anger. And it got worse. Then when the neighborhood was mostly black it got better again. The parish declined, there were not enough Catholics to keep it going and most people were living from paycheck to paycheck, some not even able to keep their homes. Many young families bought the houses and flat buildings here with government loans but were not making the money needed to maintain these old buildings."

"Dad why are you still here? Does anyone live near you?"

"No the closest is Frank, he lives in the Beverly area and Nick lives in Evergreen Park. I see them and Tom at the office every Thursday. I have breakfast with them and they discuss the business with me. It's so changed and big I can't even think about what they're doing. They do big projects, big, big projects. The three of them really turned this into a good size business. They do well together and each runs their own side of things. I'm sure they lock horns occasionally, but they seem to do just fine."

"Why don't you move closer to one of them or Bernie or someone?"

"I like it here, I have fine neighbors. They look out for me. We have a neighborhood watch program and we have three policemen and two firemen right around here. That helps."

"Why didn't you leave when you retired?"

"This is home, it was home then too for Mom and me. We didn't want to leave Doris. We just wanted to stay put. I will tell you though we started going to mass at St. Thomas Moore on 81st and California back in 73' or 74'. We joined that parish in1978, Mom was buried from there."

"Where is Mom buried?"

"Mom is buried in Holy Sepulcher Cemetery in Worth, out on 111th street and Central Ave. She is next to Paul… and I'll be on her other side someday. There is another spot there. We have one for Joe; he's a priest and pastor of a parish on the north side. He was ordained in May of 72'.

"Joey is a priest? Last time I saw him he wasn't even in school yet. I can't believe it. I missed so much."

"Would you like to go to his mass tomorrow? I'll call and find out what time he is saying mass."

"I would love to Dad, I would love to."

"Let me call there, I hope he doesn't answer the phone."

Martin walks over to the wall phone and looks for a number on the card of numbers hanging next to the phone. He dials the number, it rings, and again. "Parish office Rene speaking, may I help you?"

"Yes, I need to know what mass Father Hinelick is saying tomorrow morning, can you tell me?"

"Yes, let me go check the schedule, please hold."

Putting his hand over the mouthpiece of the phone he says, "Doris you do know how to drive?"

"Yes Dad, I do drive."

"Hello, Father Hinelick has two masses tomorrow, the 8:00 AM and the 4:30 afternoon mass."

"Thank you."

"You're welcome, good bye."

Putting the receiver back on the wall phone, he says "I have a small Ford Tempo in the garage I use it to go to mass and the store, and on Thursdays to go to work. I don't think I should drive tomorrow, too far, I'll direct you while you drive."

"That will be fine Dad, what time?"

"8:00, we have to leave at 7:00. Doris you are going to stay here tonight?"

"Yes Dad, I am going to stay if that is alright with you."

"Good, I can't believe you're here, back home. Oh I wish Mom could be here for just a little while."

"Dad after mass, I like to visit the cemetery. Would that be okay with you?"

"Sure Doris, they are at opposite ends of the map, but if you're staying tomorrow we have all day."

"Dad, what do you think Joe will say when he sees me?"

"Joe, I'm quite sure he will be surprised and just as happy as I am to see you. Joe is an extremely patient and kind man. He loves the work he does and he loves being a priest."

"Turn right here Doris. We will stay on Western Avenue for at least half an hour. I'll let you know plenty ahead of when we need to turn."

"Very good Dad, you're the guide."

"We could go the expressway but I don't drive them anymore and I am not exactly sure where we would get off."

"That's okay, I've heard about Chicago Expressways, and I'm happy to stay off of them. Actually I'm happy not to drive expressways in any big city. I sometimes drive them in Portland and that is more than enough."

"Here we are Doris. Joe has a nice Parish, he is the pastor here and has been for about seven years now."

"You got us here Dad; I hope you can direct us home as well, because I have no idea where we are."

"We're in the city, northwest side. This is St. Rachael's parish. We better go in Mass is about to begin."

"As we gather to celebrate the Eucharist we begin In the Name of The Father, and The Son, and The Holy Spirit, Amen." Joe begins the Mass.

As I look to see my brother Joe I think how terrific and slim he looks, very handsome, he looks very much as I remember Dad, but definitely thinner. His speaking voice is very calm. Dad leans over to me and interrupts my thoughts saying to me "Joe spotted us and he's wondering who my girlfriend is."

"Dad, I don't think he is paying attention to us."

"The Peace of the Lord be with you."

"And also with you."

"Now let us offer the Spirit of Christ's peace to those around us."

I turned to my left extending my right hand to Dad. He takes my hand and leaned toward me and very gently kissed me as only a father can. He spoke softly and said, "We both have peace today, thank you for coming home." We held each other in our arms as we heard "Lamb of God who takes away the sins of the world. Have mercy on us."

As we stand to go up the center isle to receive the Eucharist, Dad steps out and back to allow me to go up in front of him. We will be receiving from Joe. As our line moves forward I can hear Joe saying, "Receive the Body of Christ." and each parishioner answering "Amen." There is an elderly woman in front of me and as she answers Amen, Joe gently set the host in the palm of her hand. As I stepped up to Joe he looked at me and says "Welcome home Doris." and puts his right arm around me holding the ciborium in his left hand. He holds me tight for a moment in silence. As he stepped back I reply "Hello Joe." my eyes full of tears. He removes a single host and holding it up to me says "Doris, receive the Body of Christ."

"Amen." I answer as he lays the host in my hand.

"Dad, Receive the Body of Christ."

"Amen" I hear.

Back in our seat I take Dad's hand and squeeze.

I am overwhelmed with joy and filled with thankfulness for all my blessings.

"Receive God's Blessing in the name of The Father, and The Son, and The Holy Spirit."

All answer "Amen."

"Go now to love and serve The Lord."

"Thanks be to God."

We began singing Holy God We Praise Thy Name, as Joe leaves the Sanctuary and begins walking down the center isle. The alter servers pass and then the lectern, Joe stops takes my hand to lead me and then Dad out of Church with him between us putting his arms into ours.

"Doris you've come home! I don't know what made the time right. Mom told us many times since you left, you would come home when the time was right. You look wonderful and not as though you've been suffering I must say." "I have a glorious life, believe me. God has blessed me with the best man I could ever imagine, I lost him to cancer, Jack is gone just four months and yet he is still very much with me. When I first met Jack he very quickly became my best friend and he was my closest friend all our life together. I never knew anyone quite like him. He was always happy even, May 25, 1992, when we were told he had terminal cancer. I'll say the news took his breath away, but everyday, even that day he still smiled."

"May 25th, 92?"

"Yes?"

"That's the very day Mom died, she passed in late morning. Everyone was here. It was time. She suffered so for a few weeks. Did your husband, Jack suffer?"

"He survived over two years. He was sick but during that time he was okay too a lot. But yes when he suffered he suffered. I'm sure Mom did… I'm sorry I didn't come here sooner. Mom was right; I came home when I was ready. I wanted to be ready hundreds of times, but I never could. I never understood why until just recently. I knew now was the time to go back, to go home."

"Doris where do you live?"

"Oh Joe I have so much to tell you, I told Dad some but there is so much more. I live in Oregon, Tillamook, Oregon, in the country about 25 miles from Portland, I have four children all raised of course, two boys and two girls."

"How did you land in Oregon and how did you meet Jack?" Joe asks.

"I met Jack in London in 1953 but let me tell you how I got to London. When I left Chicago I took a train to New York. Arriving there I decided I would go on to Nova Scotia, Canada. I loved reading anything, everything about Nova Scotia when I was a little girl."

It is so cold on this train and I feel terrible. How awful do I look? I wondered as I fluffed my hair with both hands. Seeing my reflection in the window, I think, "I look better than I feel. I need to sleep."

"Everything all right Miss?" asked the conductor.

"Yes, except I am very cold, would you have a blanket I could use?"

"Of course, I'll be right up with one."

Where is this train ride taking me? I wondered will I ever go home? Where will I be sleeping tomorrow night? I wish I knew what I am doing.

"I have here a warm blanket, soft pillow and hot cup of tea for this pretty young lady."

"Oh thank you so much sir!"

"Stand up and wrap the blanket around you and keep your feet up on that foot rest. The tea will warm you-up and the blanket will keep you warm." "Thank you again sir, what do I owe you for the tea?"

"No charge."

"Thank you so much."

As the conductor walked down toward other passengers in our car I sipped the hot tea and gazed out the window. Wilderness and wilderness, this is just beautiful, nothing at all like the congested busy life in Chicago. The tea is good; I never really liked tea before, I do feel better.

"We're stopping at…" The sound of the conductor calling the stop woke me and I tightened the blanket around me as he announced stopping for fifty-five minutes. "Store's opened if you like a magazine or cigarettes or anything else. We'll be pulling out in exactly fifty-five minutes."

Oh maybe they'll have a guide or something about Nova Scotia, or a newspaper. I have to find a place to stay and a job. I get off the train and quickly enter the store; I'm cold and want to get inside. "Oh I hope I can find a place to stay!" I mumbled as I set the opened newspaper over the folded blanket covering my cold legs and feet. Good, three rooming houses have rooms available, this one says for women. Maybe that would be my best bet. I'll ask the conductor where in town this address is.

"The room is perfect, I'll take it. I'll be staying a week."

"A week, is that all?" bellowed Miss Dunn. "Oh it will be longer if I find a job right away."

"You need a job too? Go to the docks, boat docks maybe you can wait on tables down there. The men, they talk rough but they're all good men, don't be afraid, don't let them scare you, and don't bring any back here. Go see Margaret at the Sea Shell Diner, she can use you. That will be $8.00 now for your week here."

"Miss Dunn, you were right, I start at the Sea Shell day after tomorrow. I'll be staying a while. Thank you for helping me to find this job."

21

———————•— —•———————

"Margaret, I've seen this ad in the London paper a few times for a House Mom at a girl's school in London. And maybe I can take some courses at a school there. I'm thinking, maybe I could hitch a ride on a freighter to London and check out this job."

"Go over on a freighter? You, are you out of your mind Doris? These gents are all talk here in the diner, but on the sea, you won't be safe, protected, you'll be alone."

"I'll be okay. I am thinking to ask Capt. Casey, he'll watch out for me."

"Don't be a fool; he might be the worst of the lot. Take the commuter over." "I don't have the money for the commuter; I'll need all I have once I get there. I'm going to ask Capt. Casey."

———————•— —•———————

"You watch yourself now. The men they get crazy now and then and I can't be responsible for you." Captain Casey explains "You help Honey in the Galley, and stay in there, all the time! Hear me?"

———————•— —•———————

"Honey, I'll make bread. It keeps me busy. I don't think they make this much bread in a bakery."

"You do your measuring now for the morning bake." directs Honey and he continues "It will take me three sails before I am able to do this work alone again."

"Honey, I enjoy the trip, I love to cook and bake, not like this exactly, but maybe for four of five people. Honey, why do they call you Honey?"

"My name….not really. My momma, God rest her soul, she said I always hurried around her like a bumble bee looking for something sweet. She called me Honey, and I answered, so I'm Honey."

"What's your given name?"

"Masters, Chester Masters."

"Honey fits you!"

"Am I going to find you on the trip back home to Nova Scotia if you don't get the job in that girls school Doris?"

"No Honey, I'll get the job."

"Well I will miss you. You are good company here in this galley."

"Thank you Honey, you've been very nice to me."

"Do you have a place to stay until you find a job?"

"No, do you know of somewhere Honey?"

"Well, there are some rooms where most of us stay, not much, not even that clean, but not much money. If you take a room, I'll watch out for you, you know it could be rough."

"Thank you, I'll think about it. Let me see what happens when we reach England."

The measurements for the morning's bread and dinner dishes are done I am kneading the dough for tomorrow's bread thinking about Honey's offer. Where am I going to stay? I better get this job.

———————————•— —•———————————

"Oh my, you have your heart set on this job didn't you?" asks Miss Wittman as she sat across her desk from Doris.

"Yes I do, I really do!"

"Well as I said we filled both positions. I may be able to put you on in house keeping. I'll check if you'd like."

"Housekeeping, what do you mean?"

"Well the girls keep their rooms and lavatories. Housekeeping is mostly in the school buildings, infirmary, or office wing. I have three, and I need another. Would you have any interest?"

"Does it include a room?"

"We can provide a room, less money, but you do get meals with room and board."

"And classes, can I enroll in classes?"

"Not much time for classes. Maybe one, we will have to see, I don't know."

"Can I arrive today?" "Yes, if you will begin working tomorrow, I will need to have the room made up."

Chapter Three

September 15, 1952

Dear Margaret,

I am writing to let you know that I did get a job at the school for girls. I am not a house Mom but I am in house keeping, and I hate it. I have a small room here and just enough time for one afternoon class and I hope to take some college courses later.

I met a young man, Philip. He is working here in the kitchen as a cook. He is taking culinary classes in London and this is his last year. He is very sweet and we've been to a few movies together.

Honey was very nice to me on the freighter over. When he comes in tell him I said Hello.

Margaret, write if you will. I would like to hear from you. Tell Miss Dunn hello for me.

Bye for now,

Doris

December 5, 1952

Dear Margaret,

    I'm married! Yes, I am married! Phillip and I were married two weeks ago. We are both working at the school and have our rooms here, so we are not telling anyone until the end of the school year. Philip will complete his studies in May and we plan to get a flat in town. Philip said he will have no problem getting a good position right away. He really is good. I tasted his work; he brings some to me after his classes.

    A friend of Phillips lets us use his place to be together. I will meet Philip there in about an hour.

    Margaret everything is so nice. Say hello to all there and I will write soon.

Happy Holidays,

Doris

March 1, 1953

Dear Margaret

I am so sorry to hear that Miss Dunn is sick. Please bring her my best.

I have been sick too. Far different, I am expecting, next October. I wish I could be happier about this. Philip has been asked to apply for continued and further studies under some chef in Paris after graduation. He wants to go there right away. He is not happy about the baby and avoids talking about it.

We love each other and I know he will get used to the idea of being a father once we are together after the school year. I wish we could go to Paris, but I know it is not possible. Philip will have to get a job here in London.

Keep Writing,
Love,
Doris

July 1, 1953

Dear, Margaret,

    I have a new address. I am living in a room near the U.S. army base. I am working again in a diner, mostly servicemen and locals.

    Philip is in Paris. He divorced me. He said he didn't need the weight of a wife and a child. I was not able to change his mind.

    I made arrangements to stay here a while. I have a few friends who will help me. I should be alright when the baby comes in October and through the end of the year. I am praying for guidance.

    How is Miss Dunn? Is she able to walk at all yet? Let me know. Tell her I send my love.

                                    Please write,
                                        Love,
                                        Doris

September 3, 1953

Dear Margaret,

    I was so sorry to hear that Miss Dunn passed away. Thank you for keeping in touch and letting her know I was thinking about her.

    My baby will be here soon and everything is turning out much better than I thought.

    I moved again and I have a room with Mrs. Chester a widow in her sixties. The girls' school I worked at set up these arrangements. Mrs. Chester will watch the baby while I work at the diner. She has done this before for girls sent by the school.

    I never thought they would help me. I got to know this American soldier who comes to the diner. The more we talked the more he comes in. His name is Jack Stoner.

    After hearing all about Philip and the school I worked at, he contacted the school and everything happened. Jack said when you need help, ask for help, there is always help. I will be okay now, at least for a while. Tomorrow is my day off and I am glad. I am very tired. Please keep in touch.

Love,
Doris

October 25, 1953

Dear Margaret,

Scott John was born October 15ᵗʰ and weighs seven pounds. He is beautiful. I don't know who he looks like. He doesn't look like Philip and I never met any of his family, I don't know if he looks like me, but he is beautiful.

Everything is working out great with Mrs. Chester, she is so sweet. I will go back to the diner in a few weeks. She agreed to have us until spring. She said at that time I will have to move on with my life. She keeps saying, "You can't raise that boy being a waitress".

I don't think I will get too use to it here because Mrs. Chester keeps reminding me that I must set up my future.

Jack has been over to see me and Scott. (The American) I named the baby Scott John after Jack. When I told him he said his name is not John, just Jack. Oh well maybe God is telling me something.

Margaret, I look forward to your letters keep writing.

Love,
Doris

Thanksgiving Day, 1953

Dear Margaret,

     Today is Thanksgiving Day back in the United States. Jack took Scott and me to dinner at a nice Café in London. He said the base was serving turkey, but he'd rather be with us.

     No one has ever been so nice to me, but I am afraid because of Philip.

     I am sending a picture of me with Scott. Jack has a real nice camera.

     Mrs. Chester is fine and so sweet to us. I started back at the diner. The work seems harder but I am grateful for everything.

     Jack is going home for a month. He will be with his family for Christmas. I will miss him.

Keep Writing,
Love,
Doris

December 21, 1953

Dear Margaret,

    There are just a few days until Christmas and my first with Scott. I wish it could be more for him! Someday I hope we can be a complete family, a father for Scott and some brothers and sisters. We will be with Mrs. Chester on Christmas Day. Two of her children and their families are coming for the day. It will be nice to be with more people.

    I received your letter today. Thank you. I also got a letter from Jack. He is enjoying his visit home and planning his return home this summer when his tour is up. His family farms and has some livestock. He wants to build the livestock up to a business in itself.

    He will be back here before new years

    Margaret, have a Merry Christmas and Happy New Year.

Love,
Doris

January 11, 1954

Dear Margaret,

    Scott is getting so big, he weighs sixteen pounds already. Mrs. Chester tells me I am a good mother, I sure hope I am.

    The holidays were very nice; Mrs. Chester made them beautiful for Scott and me. I am glad to read in your letter that yours were nice and that your granddaughter is getting married this coming summer. I know how beautiful it is there in August. Keep writing and tell me everything. I am getting to know your family through your letters.

    Jack and I are going out for the day together, alone on Sunday. He asked Mrs. Chester to watch Scott and she was happy to. I think I am in love with Jack. I never felt this way before, not even with Philip. We are best friends and now he asked to spend a day with me. I am afraid, but happy. I will write and let you know all about it.

    You haven't mentioned Honey in your letters for a long time. How is he? Tell him I am well and say hello.

Love,
Doris

February 8, 1954

Dear Margaret,

I am beginning to think you might be right about Jack being Mr. Right. We have been out a few times alone and a few times with Scott. Jack seems to really care for Scott. I feel happy with Jack, like never before. He is a very good man. He is soon to be twenty-six years old and maybe someone a little older is better. He is very confident in what he wants to do in his life. I know I am only twenty years old and already married divorced and a mother, a lot but Jack seems to care for me and what happens to me. He is the closest friend I ever had. I don't know where this is all going but I don't want to loose my best friend.

Mrs. Chester keeps reminding me about our agreement. I think I have a place near by for the summer and a girl from school to watch Scott. I will let you know more as it all develops.

Sounds like the wedding plans are all on schedule. It sound like your daughter and son-in-law are happy with this young man. The wedding plans sound very nice. I'm happy for them; they are getting their adult life off on the right foot. I already made more mistakes than I care to think about. I'll write again soon.

Love,
Doris

March 5, 1954

Dear Margaret,

    It was nice to hear that Honey is doing well. Tell him if I need help or a ride back to Canada I'll leave a note for him at the rooming house.

    I was telling Jack about your letter and about Honey. He said I need to get all this straightened out, I am American and so is Scott, he is also British. Jack took me to his base to start the paperwork. We told the officials we are engaged so the Army will help in getting all this worked out. Tell Honey not to worry. I told them I didn't know what freighter I came over on. This could take three to six months. I hope it is done soon. Jack is scheduled to leave around August 1ˢᵗ and he is discharged around September 1ˢᵗ. He has been a good friend. He wants this accomplished as much as I do.

    Things have not changed with Jack. We seem to be rolling along.

                                  Keep in Touch,
                                        Love,
                                        Doris

Easter Sunday 1954

Dear Margaret,

Believe it or not I went to Mass today with Jack and Scott. Jack is Catholic and so am I. I've been away from the church for almost two years. I have to admit it felt good to go back.

Jack spent the day with us and Mrs. Chester. Some of her family was here too. Mrs. Chester likes Jack.

I am moving June 1st to a two room flat closer to London. I hope to get a job there.

Scott is really growing now. He doesn't even seem like a baby anymore. He'll be crawling around before I know it.

I hope your Easter was nice too. Write and fill me in on everything. I love hearing from you.

I will write soon,
Love,
Doris

May 9, 1954

Dear Margaret,

    Things are not looking good. I have a flat near London for next month but I didn't find a job or anyone to take care of Scott. I called the girls' school to inquire if someone was available to watch the baby. I can have a job there again but I can't live there with Scott. It is not enough money. I don't know what to do.

    Jack suggests I consider going back to America. He feels that Scott and I have the best chance there. I just can't go back, not now. I have a baby and I'm divorced. Jack is still working on getting my papers straightened out. I don't know what to do. I'll keep in touch. Please write soon.

                              Love,
                              Doris

P.S. Glad to hear you are all well and the wedding plans sound so exciting.

Doris.

June 27, 1954

Dear Margaret,

    I received two letters from you since I wrote and I am sorry for not writing. The wedding is only six weeks away and you so sound excited. Please keep writing with all the details. I love hearing all the news.

    It is very complicated trying to get all this paper work taken care of. Jack said it would be easier to go back to America the way I came, but I can't do that with Scott. He is determined to have it all done by the time he leaves the first week of August. Jack truly is my best friend and he really cares for Scott. When we are with him he talks about two things, getting us back to America and his plans when he returns to the family farm. He is so excited; he has such big plans for the farm. I am going to miss him; I don't know what I'll do without him.

    I am still with Mrs. Chester; she is watching Scott when I work at the diner. I could not find someone to watch Scott, and I didn't have a job. So I'm still here. Mrs. Chester has been very kind. She also feels I should go back to America. I don't know what to do. Scott will be up soon from his nap and I am helping Mrs. Chester with supper. I will write with news of the future when it happens. Don't forget to write.

Love,
Doris

June 30, 1954

Dear Margaret,

    Jack and I had a big fight earlier today. He wrote to his mother and asked her to look into some program or agency that could help Scott and me back in the States. I feel bad about getting so mad at him, but this is not his mothers business.

    I am so mad at him. He said he is trying to help as much as he can before he goes home. I told him to go home.

    The truth is I am glad he is helping me. I don't know where I would be without him. He left here mad at me telling me I better do something. I know he's right but I am still mad.

    Scott is trying to crawl around, soon I'm sure. Mrs. Chester is quiet. I don't think she feels I am being fair to Jack. After Jack left she said. "Jack's right." I don't know, I am really in trouble. I have to go for now, I will write later.

                             Love,
                             Doris

July 20, 1954

Dear Margaret,

Jack left last night. They sent him back early and he will be discharged in about two weeks. He came over the night before and I cried for two nights now. What am I going to do? Mrs. Chester feels bad too. She said to me today that I need to put together a plan.

Jack is still trying to get my American papers before his discharge. He said to tell everyone we are engaged, that will make things go faster. The truth is they couldn't be going any slower.

I did write Philip and ask if it be alright to take Scott to America. He replied, "Anywhere and don't bother me". Receiving his letter yesterday didn't make me feel any better.

Mrs. Chester has been so nice to us. She wants me to work on the papers from this end and go after Jack. She told me nothing is going to happen for me here.

Write and let me know how the wedding goes.

Love,
Doris

September 19, 1954

Dear Margaret,

I am sorry I didn't write to ask about your granddaughter's wedding. Your letter described every detail it sounds beautiful. If I close my eyes and think about your letter I feel as if I'm there. I dream of a beautiful wedding but I don't think that is really possible anymore.

Things have changed so much for me since my last letter. Back in the states Jack did everything he had to, to get me back to the United States. He was even able to get my birth certificate. I had to apply for a civilian job on the base here in England that way the army gathered all the documents I needed. Jack set all this up before his discharge and he has a guy helping him from this end. I can go back as soon as Philip gives permission for me to take Scott. He has agreed but this is going to take a few more weeks.

I got the job at the base as a clerk and Mrs. Chester watches Scott. This is more time than she wants, but she is very happy that I am getting my life in order.

When I go back to the states I will be working at the hospital in Oregon about eight miles from Jack. His mother got this job for me and they are setting me up in an apartment there. Jack has done everything for me I am very grateful. He is even paying for our transportation to Oregon. We will be there by the end of October for sure. I will write to let you know more as things develop.

Love,
Doris

October 19, 1954

Dear Margaret,

I am sitting here with all my things packed. Scott and I are leaving in a few days on a ship for the United States. I am traveling as a civilian employee of the army. We will arrive in Boston on November 4th. We will be taking a train cross country to Portland Oregon and will be on the train for six days.

Jack tells me I should be able to start work at the hospital right away. He also lined up his cousin to watch Scott while I am at work, at least for a few weeks.

I can't believe all this is happening to me and so fast, I'm not sure I even understand what is happening.

I am crazy for Jack at least for everything he is doing for me. He tells me he cares very much for me and is concerned for both Scott and me. I'm just not sure what to make of all this. I don't know what I will do if Jack is not in my future. Somehow I feel safe knowing I will be close to him.

I must tell you Scott is walking and gets into everything. Mrs. Chester has everything on high book shelves. I'm going to have to hold him on my lap from England to Oregon.

I will miss Mrs. Chester a great deal. I'll miss her like I miss my family. She has been so good to Scott and me I could never repay her. Scott just loves her and they will miss each other. I do think she will be happy to be back to her own life though.

Next time I write I will be sending the letter from my new address in the dear United States. Don't write any more until I send you my new address. Pray for us, all of us, Scott and me and Jack, also Mrs. Chester.

Love,
Doris

"Oh Jack, I'm not sure if I am happier to see you or just that I am off that train. I've been sick the entire train ride. The ship was fine, the train was awful. Scott was fine the whole trip. He sure is happy to see you Jack; if he lets go maybe I can give you a hug."

Wrapping his strong arms around me Jack whispers, "I missed you, both of you, I am very happy you are finally here."

"Me too Jack I missed you very much, but I have to tell you I am scared, this is all new and I am concerned that everything work out for Scott."

"It will work out great."

Jack was anxious to find our luggage so he could show us our new apartment, our new home. I hoped I would be happy there; I was not sure about anything. Everything was so scary and I was glad Jack was there to help me get settled. The apartment was small and old, a living room, kitchen and one bedroom, only about a quarter mile from the hospital. Jack's uncle was a doctor there and he was able to get a nurse's aid job for me. I started my job a few days later, working evening while Jack's cousin Mary Jane watched Scott. She was a senior in high school and said she would watch Scott until I found a regular baby sitter, she hoped by her Christmas break.

Everything in my apartment Jack bought, or his mother had and wasn't using. My living room and bed room furniture were from a great aunt of Jack's who died earlier that year and my table and chairs are an extra set from Jack's Mom. The dishes and pans also came from Jack's great aunt along with some of her linens. Jack thought of just about everything, he even had some food there for Scott and me to last until my first payday."

Chapter Four

***** *A LAST VISIT AND TOO MUCH MORE* *****

"Jack lived with his family on the farm west of Portland. He came to see us every week and would have us stay over night when I had Saturday evenings off. He brought us back to the apartment in time to go to work Sunday afternoon.

Early our first morning in Portland Jack picked up Scott and me for a full day at his family farm. We met his Mom and Dad, Ellen and George Stoner, very kind and generous people. It wasn't hard to see that Jack has the best of both his parents. He had three sisters, all married at that time, two were living in Eugene Oregon. Emma and her husband Pete own the local drug store, they have twin boys. Sheila taught third grade and her husband Ken is a carpenter, he still works full time. Jack's oldest sister Catherine and her husband Harry have four children and own and operate a ranch about seventy miles north. They work very hard and doubled their production early on and continued to build a very large operation. All their family is involved in the business today. Scott and I met everyone during our next two visits to the family farm. During Christmas holidays Jack took Scott and me to each of their homes.

For the next several months Jack worked very hard farming with his father and began to build up the livestock into a business all its own.

Finding a baby sitter is very difficult, by Christmas I was taking Scott to another aid's house on her days off. She watched him there and I watched her son on my days off. When we both work Mary Jane watched him or Mrs. Hunta an elderly women in the building where I lived.

By January Jack came to the city and spent time with me every evening I didn't work. He helped with everything Scott and I need whether it was hanging a picture or buying a pair of shoes. For the first time in over three years I felt safe and had a place to call home.

My feelings for Jack were overwhelming and Jack's for me. We finally slowed down and took the time to realize we were very much in love. Jack proposed on the fourth of July and we planned a harvest wedding for October 1955. We were married at St. Anne's Church and were able to have a Catholic wedding because my first marriage was not in the church and lasted only a few months. This was very important for Jack. Jack's Catholic Faith was strong and it carried him through every struggle, never forgetting to thank Our Lord for all our blessings. His Uncle Jack was a priest and there was no one he respected more.

We moved into an old farm house my in-laws bought when buying an adjacent farm shortly after the Second World War. Our other three children were born while living in that house. In 1960 we moved into our newly built ranch house with Scott a 7 year old, George 4, Margie Lynn 3 and Annie 1. We looked into Jack adopting Scott but back then it was difficult and we felt trying to work all of this out with Philip, Scott's Dad just wasn't worth the trouble that may have come up. I did have Scott's last name changed legally and he was Jack's child no less than George, Margie Lynn and Annie.

I quit working at the hospital when I married and before we knew it we had four children. I was very busy like every Mom and Jack worked long, long hours on the farm and built a cattle ranch to where we had up to eighteen thousand head at one time. Jack was involved in different Farming Associations and the Cattlemen's Association. He truly loved his work and every aspect of it. He taught all his kids and me to ride a horse, it stopped there for me but all the kids could rope and rustle cattle together and they loved it. Scott loved it the most and he is the only one directly involved in the business today. Scott runs the ranch and farm now. Jack and I bought the operation from his family while his parents were still living. Scott has five sons and one daughter and his children all love the farm. They now live in the main house, gamma and grandpa's house.

Jack and I had a wonderful life together raising the children. All of them went to St. Anne's school and County East High School. The boys both played football and they all were involved in different activities. Annie loved drama and was in all the plays while she was in high school and at Gonzaga University. She loves musicals. Annie teaches High School English in Portland, she never married. Margie Lynn is a kindergarten teacher and her husband Carl Peterson also teaches; he teaches sciences in a high school there as well as two college classes at their local Junior College. They have two daughters Jane and Alice.

Three of my children graduated from University of Oregon, and Annie from Gonzaga. George our second child is a dentist and teaches a few classes at the university. He has two children Claire and Greg. Carol, George's wife helps out in the dentist's office. They live about seven miles from me on the river. George loves to fish; this is a perfect spot for them.

Annie, my single daughter always spends extra time with me each summer and during the holidays. She wants me to go to Maine and Nova Scotia next summer. I am consisting going so I could see Margaret again, we still keep in touch, we talk a few times a year on the phone, Margaret and I that is. She will be 94 on her next birthday and does very well. Margaret moved to a small house in the same town after her husband died about twenty years ago I would love to see her again. I only knew her a few months before I left for England but we were good friends and she was a great support for me during those first three years after I left Chicago. That's funny; I didn't say left home, I said left Chicago.

My kids believe I am from Cleveland that is what I told them. I talked about Cleveland but everything was Chicago, the street names, stores, everything. My kids think Marshall Fields is in Cleveland. I never told them why I really left home. This subject was never discussed. I simply said I left because I fought constantly with my parents and it was better for all of us this way."

Dad remained silent, just looked down at his cup of coffee. The three of us stopped for a late breakfast at Daniels Restaurant before going to the cemetery. Joe told us we would get a good meal here and we did. He explained that he eats here about once a month with a few of his friends who are at parishes on the south side. "Why did you leave Doris? Mom and Dad always said being the oldest girl was tough and you needed a break. 'She'll be back when she is ready.' is the way Mom always answered our questions."

"Excuse me; I need to use the ladies room." Why did I drink so much coffee? I asked myself although I needed a few minutes to get my wits about myself. As I look into the mirror and stare at myself, I'm thinking I'm sure Dad knows but I still have to tell him. I hope he understands. And Joe, what will I say to Joe? This is not what I thought. I figured both Mom and Dad may be dead, or just Dad, but I never really figured Mom would be dead and I would have to explain to just Dad. "Well, here I go." I said out loud. I took a deep breath turned and push the door opened. As I sat down at the table I said, "Joe you asked me why I left."

"Doris, please let me talk. While you were in the rest room Dad was saying how happy he is that you are here, home again. He is sorry you didn't get to see Mom and Mom a chance to talk to you before she died but he is absolutely thrilled that you came home. Doris, I don't need to know why you left or stayed away so long. None of us ever knew. Mom and Dad never shared any of that with us. They only said you would walk in when you were ready."

"Joe, thank you, but I do need to talk to Dad about this and you too. I have thought about this now for a number of days on how I would get in touch with my family and when would be the best time. What would I say to Mom and Dad and to Jack and all my brothers and sisters especially Bernie, I know I hurt her very much when I left. I need to see her first and talk to her today, this evening if possible."

"Keep the change." Joe said to the waitress as she picked up the bill along with the thirty dollars Joe or Dad put down when I was in the bathroom. "Thanks very much for breakfast you two. The food was quite good and more than I needed to eat."

Joe rolled his chair back and stood up, he is handsome I thought and thin, he reminds me of Daddy when I left. Joe is taller than Dad, much taller. I helped Dad up and said, "Dad you look tired."

"It's been quite a day, since you came back. I slept well last night, just not long enough."

It was a short ride to the cemetery, ten minutes and Dad fell sound asleep. Joe made a right turn into the cemetery and another right then a left turn slowing down and then a stop. In the second row of stones a large light red stone cross "HINELICK".

"Dad did tell you that Paul is buried here alongside Mom?"

"Yes. Joe wait here, give me a few minutes before waking Dad and walking him over. I just need a few minutes alone." I stepped out of the car onto the snow covered grass and walked about fifty feet to the marker. The graves covered with a half inch dusting of snow I wondered if they were really there. The stone is marked off for four graves, the first reads SON Paul, Oct 6, 1969; the second reads MOTHER Mary Rose, May 25, 1992; then FATHER Martin _____; the last section is blank.

"Oh Mom, I am so sorry I let all these years pass, I missed you so, I miss you now. Dad looks terrific and I thank God I have this chance to see him and be with him. I want him to understand, I want him to forgive me. I want you to forgive me. I did a horrible injustice by not coming home sooner, much sooner. Mom I am sorry, please help Dad to forgive me and everyone, all my brothers and sisters to understand."

I pray "God thank You for getting me back while Dad is still here with us. Jesus please help me explain to him, help him to understand."

"There actually are eight graves here, four on other side of the stone. Whoever wants them can have them Dad always says 'First come first served.'"

"Is Dad awake Joe?"

"Yes, he's going to wait in the car, snow may be slippery. This end grave, next to where Dad will be is yours Doris. It's even in Dad's will. Mom and Dad said this is for you when you come home. They said even if you come home already dead, there will be a place for you here at home." Joe walks over the graves and brushes away snow first on Mom's grave then on Paul's. "Touch the grass here on each, touch the grass on both graves. Sometimes I need to feel the place where Mom rests now. I don't know why, I just do."

I stooped down and placed my palm on the grass that covers Mom's spot. The grass is hard, crisp and dry from the cold. I lift my hand to wipe my eyes and I breathed in that sweet smell, the smell of the powder or cream or something Mom used. I can't think what that smell is, but it was Mom. I turned saying "Joe smell my hand." Joe was sitting in the car with Dad; I didn't hear him walk away. I turned back and looked down. "I love you Paul. I love you Mom."

Getting back in the car I snapped my feet together trying to remove the little bit of snow on my shoes. "Thank you for bringing me here Dad and Joe."

"I don't want to get my feet cold so I just stay here in the car. Let us say a prayer." Dad continues.

Our Father, who art in heaven, hallowed be
thy name; thy kingdom come;

thy will be done on earth as it is in heaven.

Give us this day our daily bread;

and forgive us our trespasses as we forgive those who trespass against us;

and lead us not into temptation, but deliver us from evil.

Amen

Hail Mary, full of grace, the Lord is with thee;

blessed art thou among women, and blessed
is the fruit of thy womb, Jesus.

Holy Mary Mother of God, pray for us sinners,

now and at the hour of our death.

Amen

Glory be to the Father, and to the Son, and to the Holy Spirit.

As it was in the beginning, is now, and ever shall be,

world without end.

Amen

Give them eternal rest; O Lord.

And may your light shine upon them forever

May they rest in peace.

Amen

Sacred Heart of Jesus have mercy on the poor souls in purgatory.
"Doris I like to come here in the warm weather because I sometimes smell lavender."
"Lavender, that's the smell! When I touched the grass on Mom's grave I could smell lavender on my hand."
"I always think I am going to plant some at Mom's grave, maybe this year. Yes I will come this spring, so she will know you came home!"
"Where to Dad, Doris, should we go to Bernie's and surprise them? I have to get back to for Mass at 4:00."
"Later, I need a rest; we'll go to see Bernie, this evening. We'll have dinner early and then go. Is that alright Doris? Of course, it's fine. Joe drive back to your place and Dad will direct me home from there."

"Could I tag along tonight? After Mass I'll stop at the house and pick-up you two, about five thirty if that is alright with you?"

"Yes, I would like that very much Joe. We'll have something for you to eat."

"Don't worry about me eating, I'll get something. I'll call you from home as soon as I am ready to head to Dad's No, better yet I'll call Jim, he's at the house, he told me he'd be in all day studying. Maybe I can impose on him to say the four o'clock. I'll stop at this gas station and call him."

"Joe, get me a Seven-Up while you're in there, would you please?"

"Sure Dad, anything for you Doris?"

"No, I'm good, thank you Joe."

"Father Sullivan will say the four o'clock for me. We'll go back to your house Dad and you can lie down for a couple hours."

"That'll be great, you and Doris can visit and Doris will tell you all she has shared with me last night."

"Joe, I am going to have a cup of tea, would you like one?"

"Yes I would like something and tea sounds good."

"Dad looks wonderful, he seems really healthy."

"He is in good shape. He takes care of himself and we don't worry that much about him. He has a few neighbors who look out for him. They shovel the snow, cut the grass and other small jobs around here. He also keeps something of a routine. He plays cards every Monday and Friday with some other retired men at the church he goes to, St. Thomas Moore and he has breakfast every Thursday with Nick, Frank and Tom. They now own and operate the business Dad started. I get out here about once a week. Everyone calls, stops in or has Dad to dinner he is out two or three nights every week. I take him to lunch on Saturdays sometimes, when I can get away from the parish. Dad's health is really pretty good, no major problems, Annie takes him grocery shopping every couple weeks and he stops for the few extra things in between."

"That's good Joe; it sounds as though Mom and Dad had a nice retirement together."

"Yes, I must say they have. When Mom got sick though that was very hard on both of them, she suffered for a few months, and Dad just couldn't deal with that. But not long after Mom died he began to play cards with his friends again and got into the routine he still follows. He goes to Mass almost everyday. Bad weather will hold him back more than anything, especially snow. He does drive to most anywhere but never at night, if he is going to someone's later in the day they pick him up and bring him home."

"Well it certainly looks as though, and with what you're telling me Dad is doing just fine for someone his age. Eighty-six he is doing great. I'm happy just to see him again."

"Doris, sit down, a watched pot never boils."

"Okay Joe, Dad had some pound cake last night, let me cut a few pieces for us to have with our tea."

"I love pound cake and Sara Lee's is always good."

"Joe, wait for the tea!" I snapped as I watched Joe take a bit of his cake. "Yes ma'am!"

"Oh Joe, I didn't mean that, have more there is lots of cake here."

"Doris, I'm just teasing you, come on sit down, relax."

"Joe the water is boiling let me fill the tea pot and then we will talk."

Joe reaches onto the table and takes my right hand. "Doris, Doris I really didn't think I'd ever see you again. I don't remember much of anything from before you left, a little, but I do remember how sad and upset Mom and Dad were when you left. They thought you'd be home soon, they hoped for Christmas that year."

"Joe, I must talk to Dad alone before we go to see Bernie this evening. We talked about my life since I left, but not a word about my leaving. This is very hard for me even harder than I thought it was going to be."

"Doris, about six months after Mom died Dad talked to me about his death and funeral and how he wanted things to be handled. He reminded me that the grave next to him was for me or Doris, whoever died first."

"Oh, Joe, please don't tell me all this!"

"Doris, I told Dad that all his and Mom's prayers did not go unanswered and that you were probably very happy somewhere with a family of your own. I told him all of us are doing fine and I was sure Doris was doing fine as well; after all she was raised by the same parents. I so wish I could have convinced him, I wish I believed it myself."

"You were right, most of their prayers were answered Joe. I do have a wonderful, happy life, but I should have come home a long time ago Joe.

"I told you Mom always said 'Doris will come home when she is ready'. Well she was right on target. You are ready aren't you?"

"Yes, Joe I am ready and I am very nervous. But it is time!

"Doris, earlier today I said I didn't know why you left. That is not true, I do know. That same day, Dad told me you were pregnant and they were both very upset with you. Dad said they were both so shocked and he didn't even know what to think. He said they pressed you to tell them who the father was. They suspected one guy you dated once. He said you would not tell them."

"No I wouldn't Joe. I did not want the boy to know or Mom and Dad to know who he was."

"Why not Doris, why didn't you let Mom and Dad help you?"

"Oh Dad, you're up already, you just laid down thirty minutes ago?"

"Yes Doris I did fall asleep but I could hear you two talking and I am not used to having anyone around when I sleep, so little noises wake me."

"Well, sit down and join us, I'll make a fresh pot of tea."

Joe moves around the small round table and sat against the wall and Dad sat where Joe was. "Doris, I didn't want to hear your conversation with Joe. I don't need to know why you left. I just don't want you to think I was eavesdropping."

"Dad, I'm sorry, I want to talk to you about this! I love you. I was just telling Joe that I refused to tell you and Mom who the father of my baby was. I also never told him I was pregnant."

"Times then were far different than they are now Doris or maybe they're not so different now. But anyway your mother and I talked everyday for at least two or three weeks about this and she got madder each day."

"Mom made arrangements for me to stay with her cousin at a girl's school and convent in Springfield and I would be home for the next Christmas. Well I was graduating in a few weeks and planning on going to college that September but I wanted no part of Mom's plan. I was enrolled for the fall at Chicago Teachers College. That was what I wanted to do and having a baby was just about the worst thing I could do. I had enough babies to last me a life time I thought. After all, Mom was expecting her tenth child and I thought you were both crazy. I was seventeen Joe. Everything would be worked out once I got to Springfield, an adoption arranged and we would tell people I was attending a college in Springfield. But I wanted to go to Chicago Teachers College, and staying home was out of the question. You and Mom were not happy about any of this and you had an entire plan worked out. I was crazy unhappy about the whole mess. And to tell you the truth, I was embarrassed about being pregnant, I never even told my friends. I only confided in Maureen Potter, and the only thing she knew was that I was pregnant and about your plan and how I felt about it. I felt like I was at the absolute lowest point in my life. I could only see how this mess affected me. I knew you and Mom were embarrassed but I was not about to ruin my life and do what you wanted. I remember crying and thinking they don't care about me, just about the embarrassment. I didn't want this and I didn't know what to do."

"Doris, I don't remember talking or considering any other options."

"Dad, there were no other options at that time. And what you and Mom worked out was truly the best solution; I couldn't and wouldn't see it at that time."

"Doris what happened? How did you work this out?"

"Joe, it was awful, worse than awful, it was a real live nightmare!"

"Doris, please don't!"

"Daddy, I have to tell you, I can't change the past as hard as I tried I can't change the past. Ignoring it hasn't worked either; I've been doing that for forty-five years."

"But telling us all about it, bring all this up again won't change things either."

"Joe, you're right, explaining all of this won't change the past but it will begin to fill in that black hole in my heart, in my soul that is always present and has been for more than forty four years. I got pregnant in late February that year and I knew almost immediately I prayed for a miscarriage. It hurts me to say that today or even thinking of it. But the truth is I did pray for a miscarriage constantly. I confided in Maureen, she knew something was bothering me. She was a true friend and never stopped telling me to talk to my parents, 'They will understand.' she said 'They won't be happy but they will understand.' She was right! Later, years later every time I looked back I knew Maureen was right, I remembered you did understand and you didn't like it but you did understand. Well as the weeks passed and I didn't miscarry I knew I had to tell Mom and when I did she almost blew the roof off the house. Of course we had lots of words about all this that I don't believe either of us really meant; never the less we said them. Then Mom told you and you certainly weren't very happy. I remember you telling me to please understand and listen to your mother. 'What she is doing is best for you and your baby.' I paused. I couldn't even think or talk. Daddy, I'll never forget those words 'your baby' everyone even Maureen and the doctor I went to referred to 'the baby' never 'your baby'. Well, after that Dad, you and I never talked about my pregnancy again. Everything was handled by Mom, poor Mom; she was expecting Annie at that time. She was trying to help me and I was so wrapped up in myself I twisted her help into believing it was just a way out of her embarrassment. Well I hated the idea of leaving shortly after graduation for Springfield. I knew about this girl from Longwood, Joe that's where I went to high school."

"I know Bernie went there too."

"This girl she graduated the year before me and she got pregnant in her senior year and had a miscarriage. But the story going around school was that she had an abortion. Well I knew her a little and where she lived. I got in touch with her and confided in her. She denied having an abortion but did give me the name of a woman to see. I did see this woman and she had me see a` particular doctor. I told her I already saw a doctor and she said that's fine, now go see this doctor. She had me see him after his regular hours, all his nurses were gone. It was only him and me. He examined me and told me to go back to see this woman on Friday morning early. I didn't pay him anything. I paid her on Friday. I'll never forget sixty-five dollars. To this day every time I hear those three words together, sixty-five dollars, I think of that awful day. She took me to this room in her basement and preformed the abortion.

I couldn't believe what I had done. I rested there until late in the afternoon and then I took a cab downtown to the train station and got on a train for New York. My plan was to stay there for a few weeks then return telling you I had a miscarriage."

"Oh, Doris, why did you ever do all this?"

"Daddy, I felt horrible! It was absolutely horrible! I felt terrible; I was sick and so tired. I did sleep some on the train and when I arrived in New York I knew I couldn't go back to Chicago in a week or two. I knew I could never face you and Mom about what I did.

There was a train leaving that night for Nova Scotia Canada and I loved reading about Nova Scotia so I bought a ticket for that train and never came back. I knew I could never tell you or even Maureen, I knew she would never understand. What I did and what happened was horrible and I have regretted it everyday of my life since."

"Doris, I'm so sorry, Mom and I never ever thought something like this happened. We never even thought you may have considered this."

"Dad, Doris probably didn't know what this really meant at the time."

"Yes I did Joe. Joe there is no way to soften this. I knew what I was doing and I did it. When I was being readied for the abortion I knew this was wrong. I wanted to jump up and run but I was even too afraid to do that. Joe, I had lots of choices and I kept making the wrong ones, mostly because I didn't want to face the ones I already made."

Dad is sitting looking down at the table; both of his hands are in Joe's. I am holding Joe's other hand. I take my right hand and softly place it over Dad's and Joe's. "Dad, maybe it would be better if you too could go to your grave never knowing all this."

"Doris!"

He takes my hand with both his. "Daddy, please understand, I'm glad you're here to hear this story and I wish with all my heart Mom was still alive. Dad it was time for me to come home."

"Doris, I am sad, sad about what you went through, about all the years lost. I am sad that this awful memory is what you live with everyday."

"Dad"

"Doris please wait, Let me talk, I am thrilled to see you again, to have you home. Please know how much I love you." He pulls his hands away, leans on the table and stands coming toward me, he holds me in his arms, like I have never been held before. "I love you, thank you for coming home."

Both of our eyes are filled with tears as I squeeze, my Dad saying "I love you too Dad"

Joe suggested having dinner at Foxes in Oak Lawn before going to see Bernie. No sooner did he suggest this and the phone rang. Joe answered. "Hello --- Bernie we were just planning to have dinner at Foxes and then stop for a visit with you and Tom. Will you be home a little later? --- Sure Bernie, meet us there at five. Is that okay Dad?"

"Of course"

"Great Bernie, we'll see you at Foxes!"

"Joe, please tell her we would rather stop and visit with her first and then go to dinner." "Bernie, would it be alright if we stop at your place first, before dinner? --- Great Bernie --- That will work. Bye"

"Dad, Bernie said to come now and we can have a glass of wine at their place before we head over to Foxes."

"She is going to need more than a glass of wine when I walk in!"

"Doris would you rather not?"

"Oh no Daddy, I'm as ready as I can get. I am nervous but you two made this very easy and you both are so accepting. I need to see everyone and meet Anne. I never met Anne. I can't wait to see Jack too and all of my brothers and sisters."

"Then I guess you need to meet Terry."

"Terry?"

"Yes, you never met Terry, he's the baby born a year after Annie."

"Oh my, I have another brother?"

"You sure do."

"What does he do? Tell me about Terry."

"Terry is just twelve and a half months younger than Annie. He was born September 30th 1952 and was somewhat spoiled by every one in this family. Well if you ask me Doris, Terry and Annie were both pretty much spoiled!" "Joe, I'm sure you know the youngest always get everything."

"Well you're both somewhat right. By the time they got to high school we had a little more money and they benefited, not that the rest of you suffered much. I am truly thankful we always had an income, there was always work in the business and we always had at least what we needed."

"Terry! Tell me about Terry!"

"He is single, never married and teaches Literature, English and History at Marist High School, a Catholic Boys High School on the south side. He lives alone in a nice small condo in Palos Hills and has a cabin, a year round cabin up on a river in the Couhly Region of Wisconsin. He loves to fish and read. He's there all summer and long weekends. Someday maybe he'll take a teaching job in that area. But he says no, it is to isolated to be there all the time. He dates some and claims he would like to marry someday, but nothing yet, I don't think he has ever come close to marrying or feeling that way about any girl."

"I can't wait to meet Terry too."

"Can you stay for a few days Doris? We will get everyone over here to see you."

"Dad I could stay a few days. I would have to leave by Thursday though, my closest friend Colleen, her granddaughter is getting married on Friday and I can't miss the wedding. I promised her I'd be back in time."

"Wonderful, let's start by visiting with Bernie tonight."

"Great Dad, just give me a few minutes and I'll be ready."

"Okay Doris. Joe, are you ready?"

"Yes, Pop I need to get home tonight so I'll ask Tom to give me a ride after dinner. Dad, you lock everything up and I'll warm-up the car."

———————

"Here we are at Bernie's, Doris why don't you wait in the car and Joe and I will go in first."

"Dad, I walked in on you and we both walked in on Joe. I'll go in with you alright?"

I get out of the back seat and help Dad out of the front. Looking around I think it's a nice house in the center of the block, neat as a pin. We walked up the drive way to a side entrance; Joe presses the bell while Dad and I follow behind. Bernie opens the door and holds the storm door for Joe and Dad. "Hi Joe and Dad, it's good to see you guys! Oh hello, why I'm Bernie, Joe's sister."

"And so am I, yours too!"

"Doris? Oh no, you can't be! Are you Doris?"

"Yes, Bernie, believe it or not it is me, Doris."

"Doris? Doris, where have you been? Oh my! Oh my! Doris where have you been? You look just like Aunt Helen. Oh my God, I have to sit down I'm shaking all over. Tom! Tom! Come up here. Tom's down in the den finishing a puzzle he will laminate for one of the grandkids. Tom!"

"Bernie, I'm coming, are you alright?"

"No, I'm not alright."

Bernie is sitting at the kitchen table and Dad walks around to sit down as Tom walks up just a few steps from the lower level saying "Bernie?"

"Tom, come up here and meet your sister in law Doris Hinelick. It is Hinelick isn't it?"

"No, it's Stoner, Doris Stoner!"

"Doris Stoner! Hi. I'm Tom Michaels." He had paused on the top step and now putting out his right hand to me steps up into the kitchen.

"Tom, I'm Doris Stoner, Bernie's oldest sister. I'm quite sure you heard of me."

"Why yes, and it is nice to meet you, finally meet you."

"Tom, can you believe this? I never thought I would ever see you again Doris! I thought you were dead! Why didn't you ever call? Where have you been? Don't tell me you have been around here all this time. Have you?"

"No, I live in Oregon."

"Oregon, Illinois?"

"No Oregon State, near Portland."

"What does your husband do?"

"Jack, my husband is dead now. We farm; one of my sons runs the farm now."

"Doris, my heart is going a thousand miles a minute."

"So is mine Bernie."

"When did you get home?"

"Last night. I just came to the house and didn't know what I would find. I was surprised Dad was in the same house and even has the same phone number. Dad took me to mass at Joey's church and Joe and I got reacquainted. The three of us went to the cemetery after mass. I can't believe my little brother is a priest! There are just so many things I didn't know. I still have never met Annie or Terry. I'm looking forward to meeting them and seeing everyone."

"Please, everyone sit down. Tom, get another chair and we well all sit around the table."

"How about a drink, would everyone like a drink?"

"Yes Tom," answers Bernie "we will have a drink, wine, we'll all have wine."

"You too Doris, would you like a glass of wine?"

"Yes, of course, Tom that would be nice, I would love some."

"Doris, I don't even know where to start."

"Why don't you start by telling me about you and Tom and your family? I would love to hear all about your family."

"Yes but first I want to know about you Doris, everything!"

"Alright, I will start. Dad and Joe already heard all of this earlier; Dad heard it a few times. I met Jack, my husband in England in 1953. He was a serviceman stationed there and I was a waitress in a café near the U.S. base."

"Oh this sounds like a romance novel!"

"Well, sort of Bernie, but it didn't seem like a romance novel when I was living through it."

"I'm sorry for interrupting, go on Doris, please."

"Jack realized I was American and he always made sure to sit at my table whenever he came into the cafe. Once he found out I was getting a divorce and was due to have a baby in a few months, he wanted to help me get back to the United States. Well at the time I had nowhere in the United States to go and I was hoping that Philip and I could get back together once the baby came."

"So you were married to Philip first?"

"Yes."

"Tell us about Philip and how you met him."

"Well, when I arrived in England I took a job at a girl's school and Phillip worked there as a chef. He was studying culinary art at that time in London. Well we fell in love, we were both very young. I was alone in England and that was all there was to it. After I got pregnant Philip was offered an opportunity to study in France under a chef and he made no qualms about the fact that this opportunity was important and the baby and I were not, so he left and a divorce quickly followed. And he wanted nothing to do with our child. He left and was in France months before Scott was born.

Well anyway Jack continued to come into the café and help me get all my papers straightened out so I could eventually get back to the United States… and Jack died six weeks ago just about two and a half years after discovering cancer."

"Doris, it is comforting to know that you have such a wonderful life. Your story as told is one to be envy. But with all do respect, you neglected to tell us just why it is that you left and where you went!"

"Bernie, that wasn't necessary!"

"Dad, Doris left forty some years ago, she walked out on you and Mom and all of us. Not a single word in all that time and today she walks into my house and lays out this beautiful story book life story of hers. You want to know the truth Dad, I don't know what to think, Doris I don't know what to think or feel. I thought of someday finding you, thousands of times I thought of it. I have told you off in my mind time after time. And now you're here telling this pretty little story and I should feel good? Well guess what? I don't like it, I don't feel good, and it makes me sick. Excuse me, if you don't mind."

"No of course." I replied as Bernie pushed her chair away from the table, turned and went upstairs. We all flinched at the slam of the door from the top of the stairs. "I'll go up and talk to her, I'll try to explain." I said as I stood to go up stairs.

"No, I'll talk to her. Sit down Doris please, please sit down, I'll be down in a few minutes."

"Tom, I'm sorry, I'm sorry about this. Please tell Bernie I will explain everything to her and I understand that she has every right to be mad and frankly I would be too."

"I'll be back shortly." Tom said as he disappeared up the stairs.

"Doris, Bernie will be alright, just giver her a little time."

"I know Joe. I expected this reaction to my return. I just want Bernie to understand. I want all of you to understand."

Joe continued "Bernie's not the only one who will react this way to your return and it may take a while for some to accept it, but I believe in time everyone will get through this."

Dad, Joe and I sat silently for what seemed like such a long time. Then Joe began "You know I'm thinking maybe it would be better if Dad and I talked to everyone first before you do Doris. Give them each a little time to absorb all of this."

"Yes, yes I agree that would be better, much better than this!" Dad confirmed.

"Well this certainly didn't work out very well and I don't want to hurt anyone anymore than I already have." "Doris these things are all wounds. All of us have them but I don't think any of us really thought we would ever have to deal with them. We were pretty much resolved to never knowing anything about you, whether you were alive or dead. We knew nothing at all about you. Our worst fear was to find out you were dead all this time. But maybe the worst is actually dealing with your return, you being well, having a full, normal life. I have to say it angers me some also. You knew for forty some years where we were yet you never called. We had no clue to your whereabouts, your name, if you were dead or alive, nothing. We even tried to find you, always with out Dad's and Mom's knowledge of course and yet never a clue, nothing as if you vanished."

Tom just came down from talking to Bernie.

"We're not going to go to supper, Bernie would rather you went and she said to tell you Dad that she would talk to you later in the week. …. So"

"Okay Tom, do you think I should talk to her now."

"No Dad, she'll call you later in the week."

Backing out of the driveway Dad said "Just go home, I have some soup we'll eat."

"Dad, I'll drive to my place and then Doris will drive the two of you home."

"Fine, Joe. That will be just fine."

"Joe, my home is in Oregon, this is not my home anymore. I made a number of very poor choices many years ago, because of those choices this is happening to me today. I am sorry for the bad choices I made, but I am not sorry for my life. I am very happy! I have a great life. I shed many tears over the last forty years because of all these mistakes, but even a flood of tears cannot change the past. I wanted the past to end, to be gone but dealing with it sometimes takes more than we can do. I needed to come back, I need to see each of you and talk to each of you. It's hard for me but as I see now even harder for you." We rode the rest of the way to Joe's pretty much in silence. Asking us in, Dad answered Joe,"We both just want to move along." Giving me a super hug, Joe whispers "I love you. Please be very patient. There is lots of healing necessary for all of us."

"Thank you Joe, I love you too."

———————————•—•— —•—•————————————

"Good morning Doris"

"Good morning Dad. How are you this morning?"

"Good, I feel good. How did you sleep?"

"Not well. Dad, I'm going to head home today. Joe is right. It would be better for you and Joe to talk to everyone."

"Doris, are you sure?"

"Yes Dad, I am."

"Doris you haven't seen your brothers and sisters since you were kids. Do you want to wait longer?"

"Dad, it was most important that I see you. I did and you could not have been kinder to me. Thank you."

"Doris"

"Dad, it would be better for everyone else to hear my story and get used to the idea. I'll come back for a visit in a month or so."

"Doris, promise me you'll come back!"

"I'll be back, for sure. I promise. And when I come back, I'll bring lavender and the two of us will plant some on Mom's grave."

"Let's have some breakfast, what do you say?"

"Yes, sounds good. My flight leaves in about four hours."

———————————•—•— —•—•————————————

"Doris I think your cab is here."

"Okay, I'll be right there."

"Doris, I am going to miss you all over again."

"Dad I will be back for a visit next month. You and I will talk, I'll call you tomorrow, okay?"

"Okay"

I reach out and Dad and I hug. "Thank you Dad, so much, for everything. I love you."

Kissing my cheek, slowly says, "I love you Doris."

We hold tight for a minute and hear the beep of the cab horn. "Dad, I have to go. Thank Joe for everything and tell him I will call. Explain to Bernie and I will give her a call after I talk to you. Love you Dad, and thank you."

"God be with you Doris."

Dad moved from the porch as the cab pulled away and we both were drying our eyes.

"What time is your flight?" asks the cabbie.

"12:15"

"No problem, we have plenty of time."

This area has changed so much; I would never know it is the neighborhood I grew up in. I thought as we headed for O'Hare. But Dad, the same gentle quiet man, he is just as I remembered, but older, much older.

<hr>

"Hello"

"Hello Scott"

"Hi Mom, when did you get home?"

"Just a little while ago, about 30 minutes."

"How was your trip?"

"It was nice, very nice."

"Scott, I would like to invite you and Mary Beth to come to dinner on Sunday at 2:00. I am inviting the four of you and your mates. I want to talk to all of you about my trip and some business I am taking care of. Everyone else can make it, I hope you can too."

"Mom, hold on I will check with Mary Beth but I am sure there will be no problem, we will be at your house at two."

"Wonderful I will see you Sunday Scott."

"Can we bring something, desert or something?"

"No, just bring your attention span."

"Okay Mom."

"Good bye Scott, I will talk to you soon."
"Bye Mom."

———————●——— ———●——————

"Hi Gram"
"Well hello Claire, how are you?"
"I'm good Gram. How was your trip?"
"I didn't expect to see you back this soon!"
"Well I didn't know exactly how long my business would take."
"Well it was quick!"
"Oh I have much more to take care of so I will be going back in a few weeks. Claire, I'm glad you stopped. I was going to call you tonight and ask you to come over on Saturday to help me do some of the food preparations for my Sunday dinner."
"What dinner?
"I invited the adults, including your parents for Sunday dinner. I need to discuss some of business with them. Could you help me out on Saturday?"
"Sure Gram. What time do you need me?" "Come at noon, I'll have lunch for us. Claire, how are you feeling, is everything going well for you right now?"
"Gram, I've been feeling alright. I haven't been sick at all for a about a week.
"Is your father aware of your condition?"
"No, Mom and I have not told him, Mom doesn't know you know about this either."
"What about the boy, the young man, the baby's father?"
"No nothing, we haven't even talked, I avoid him."
"Claire you need to talk to him and your father!"
"Gram please, you don't understand how hard this is."
"I do know, you need to tell them and soon!"
"Okay Gram no more talking about this. I'll see you Saturday."
"Good because I could use your help. I love you Claire."
"I love you too Gram, bye."

I watch as Claire pulled away in the Acclaim I gave her after Jack died. I liked driving that car. Jack's Town Car is so big, I never liked driving big cars I thought I really should sell it and buy a smaller car. I sat down in the den with a yellow pad on a clipboard, pen in hand to outline all I need to include in my talk to the kids this coming Sunday. I don't even know where to begin, I think as I look down at the yellow paper, nothing. I start just as I started most of my work when I was in school. In the upper left hand corner I began with "J.M.J".

Chapter Five

Making some notes but little progress when I heard a car pulling up the drive, I get up and walk to the front window for a look. Now, who is coming up the walk? I ask myself. He has a beautiful leather coat and he looks good in that tweed Irish cap. Well let me see what he is selling. I open the door as he approaches the porch. "Hello, what can I do for you?" I look closer as he removes his hat.

"Hello, are you Doris Stoner?"

"Yes, I am, how can I help you?"

"I'm your brother, Terry Hinelick."

"Terry, you're Terry?"

"Yes"

I open the door. "Please come in."

"Thank you Doris"

"Are you really Terry, my brother Terry?"

"Yes, I am."

"Terry, what are you doing here? How did you find me? I never even met you before. Oh give me a hug, please give me a hug!" I put my arms up and out to hug him. He was apprehensive and shy but I gave him a hug like a great old friend.

"Doris you're practically squeezing the life out of me!"

I release him hesitantly.

"I can't believe, no I'm so surprised and happy you are here. Please come in, take off your coat and let me look at you!"

"Doris you do look like Aunt Helen. Joe told me that Bernie said you look like Aunt Helen and she was right, you do!"

66

"How is she, Aunt Helen I mean, are she and Uncle Frank still living?" "Uncle Frank died in the early 60s and Aunt Helen just about a year ago. You look more like Aunt Helen than Monica and Julie look like her, her own kids!"

"How are they?"

"Fine, both are doing well."

"Tell me about them later. I want to hear about you first, tell me about you. Come over here please and sit right here in the kitchen. Would you like some coffee or tea, a soft drink maybe?"

"Yes, coffee or tea which ever you would like, I enjoy both."

"I'll make some fresh coffee." Grabbing the filter and the coffee container I ask Terry, "You must have talked to Dad or Joe maybe Bernie yesterday, whom did you talk with about me?"

"Yes I talked with Joe. We keep in touch and talk often almost daily."

"Joe was wonderful to me and maybe not completely honest about how he felt when he saw me. He was truly a gentleman. He could not have treated me nicer."

"Joe is the best! He is my best friend and a great big brother."

"Do you and Joe get together often?"

"Oh yes absolutely, I see Joe quite often, we have many common interests and common friends. And we are both single, he permanently, me maybe not, I guess time will tell." "Do you have a love interest Terry?"

"Not at this time. I do date some but no one of great interest."

"Dad told me you are a teacher and you have an apartment and a cabin in Wisconsin somewhere. He said you love teaching."

"Yes I do. I teach English and History at a boy's high school in the city. I also do counseling there and I am working on my doctorate and will be done in about sixteen months."

"Where are you studying?"

"I went all through college at Loyola University in Chicago and I am still there studying."

"That is wonderful; my baby brother will have a doctorate degree. Are there any other doctors in the family?" "Yes, Joe has his doctorate in theology and Tom, Bernie's husband is an eye doctor an Optometrist. Both Jack and Annie's husband Tom Schwartz are lawyers. That's it, no more!"

"Where do they practice?"

"Tom has a family and small business law practice in the Chicago area. Jack is a States Attorney and planning to retire soon."

"Terry, tell me about Terry. Everything there is to tell, please tell me everything. I need to hear everything!"

"Well I am the youngest of ten kids, no eleven kids. I always say I have nine brothers and sisters, one who is now dead."

"To be honest with you for the past thirty years, at least I didn't tell anyone about you. I never even knew you and couldn't tell people anything about you. I just eliminated you from the family. Before that, when I told people I had ten brothers and sisters, they always asked questions about you that I couldn't answer and I didn't know anything, so then I just told people I had nine siblings, believe me it's been a lot easier."

"That makes me feel sad, I'm not sure why, because I've been telling people I have no family. Oh, Terry, I really don't know what to say or what to even think about all of this, the mess I made by never coming home, by never contacting Mom and Dad."

My eyes are full and Terry's too, a little. "I let forty some years go by and never once tried to contact my family. I wanted to call, to talk to Mom and Dad but I never did, I just kept putting off calling. I never even contacted a friend of mine from home to inquire about my family. I thought about it. I'm sure I could have trusted Maureen Potter, she was my best friend. I know she would have communicated with me and not let my family know. But I would have had to tell her I aborted my baby. I just couldn't tell her that, I couldn't tell anyone."

Terry leaned back in his chair, tilted his head down. "You aborted your child? Joe explained to me that you left because you were pregnant and weren't happy with the arrangements Mom and Dad made for you!"

"Yes I did and I wasn't happy with Mom's plan. I got pregnant late winter of my senior year. I wanted to go to Chicago Teachers College the next fall, but Mom and Dad wanted me to go and stay at a girl's home in Springfield. My baby was due late in November and I couldn't stand the thought of not going to college at CTC."

"CTC?"

"Yes, Chicago Teachers College."

"Doris, Joe didn't tell me you ended your pregnancy, I just thought you gave up your baby for adoption. I just wasn't expecting you to say that Doris!"

A sudden knock at the kitchen door breaks the tension of our conversation and moves it right into an uncomfortable anxiousness we both cannot hide. "Come in" I yelled turning toward the door leading out to the side drive. "Come in Scott, there is someone here I want you to meet."

"Hi Mom"

Terry stands up as Scott walked into the room and steps toward him. Terry, this is my oldest son, Scott Stoner. He is my first born, from my first marriage. Scott, I would like you to meet Terry Hinelick, Terry is your uncle, my youngest brother."

Scott holds out his right hand to greet Terry and turns his head toward me saying, "This is my uncle, your youngest brother? Is there another one or more than one?" Turning back and shaking hands Scott asks, "I'm sorry, is it Terry?"

"Yes it is, Scott it is nice to meet you."

"Thank you! And it is nice to meet you as well. Mom, maybe you could explain!"

"Scott, I plan to explain all of this and more on Sunday to you, George and your sisters."

"Does this have something to do with your trip to Chicago?"

"Yes it does."

"Mom, I'm going to the post office, do you need anything in town?"

"No Scott, nothing at all. Thank you though".

"Terry it is a surprise to meet you, will I be seeing you again anytime?"

"Scott, I hope so, I would like to meet the rest of the family."

"Good, then I will be seeing you again, on Sunday maybe?"

"No, I'm afraid not, I am heading back to Chicago tonight. Hopefully we can visit another time soon." "Scott, I will explain everything later, have a nice trip to town."

"Okay Mom, nice to meet you Terry."

"You too, take care."

I close the door as Scott walks down the drive to his truck. As I turn back toward Terry, he asked, "Your children don't know about us do they?"

69

"Nothing, except for Scott, and he only knows what he just found out here in the last two minutes. Terry, please sit, I'll pour coffee for us. Do you use sugar and cream?"

"Just cream thank you."

"I have much to tell you Terry. I wasn't planning on you dropping by, any more than Dad expected me last Saturday."

I'm quite sure you surprised him and Joe, and from what I understand you really caught Bernie off guard."

"Poor Bernie, she is really mad at me, I can't say I blame her, when I left she was 14 and we were very close. I know I hurt her terribly. Unless Joe told her she still does not know why I left. He didn't tell you Terry so I doubt if he told her."

"Why did you leave and never call?"

"It was absolutely the lowest time in my life."

"I got pregnant in February of my senior year in high school. I wasn't even dating this guy, so it was very easy for me to keep the fathers name to myself. Late April, early May I told Mom, she told Dad and the next thing I knew I would be going to the girl's home in Springfield a few days after graduation. Mom and I fought about this just about everyday. All I wanted was to be able to start college in September. I wanted the whole thing to just go away. I prayed for months that I would have a miscarriage."

"Oh Doris, this must have been awful, a terrible time for you."

"Yes, it was awful but I made it much worse. Let me finish, I managed to make arrangements with the neighborhood abortionist and leave for two weeks, come back and tell Mom I miscarried while I was away."

"Where were you going to go?"

"I did not want Mom and Dad to know what I did, I thought this would work. The fact of the matter is after the abortion I couldn't believe what I did. I knew before hand I should not go through with it and once I was at this woman's house I was so scared I let it all happen; She opened the door leading to the basement, I followed her descending the stairs everything looked gray. 'Be careful little one' she said 'the railing is wobbly.' I'll never forget, I did nothing to stop it. When I left her house I ran and I just kept running. I believed I could never face Mom and Dad again. I kept going until I ended up in Nova Scotia where I worked for about six weeks and then took a freighter to England where

I met and married Philip Masters. Soon I was expecting a baby and he took off. After he left I was working as a waitress and I met Jack Stoner, a soldier from home. He was so kind to me and after Scott was born he helped me get my papers straight so I could go back to the United States and bring Scott with me. After his discharge that summer he continued to get everything straightened out and I returned to the United States in November that same year. Scott was thirteen months old when we arrived here. Jack found an apartment and job for me as well as a baby sitter to watch Scott while I was at the hospital where I worked. Jack and I married the next fall and had three more children, George, Margaret Lynn and Annie. We raised our children right here on this farm just where Jack was raised." "This is absolutely beautiful here Doris and looks like a wonderful place to live and raise a family."

"Yes Terry and I love it here on this farm, it's home for me, my home I love and have since I married Jack."

"I can see how the old neighborhood in Chicago doesn't quite compare to this."

"Terry, that's not it at all. The second biggest mistake in my life was that I believed I could not go home, that I would not be welcome. I wanted to go home. I wanted to see Mom and Dad and all of you. I was afraid, embarrassed, and mostly ashamed of what I did. I thought about coming back many, many times and telling Mom and Dad that I did have the baby and I had him adopted. Jack wanted me to contact my parents but he felt the truth was the only way to accomplish this. "You have to get out from under this, don't make this terrible situation worse." He told me numerous times. Jack was a man of faith, he believed and lived his faith every moment of his life. He called on God for everything from a little breeze to cool his face on a hot July afternoon to helping him accept and bare the pain of the cancer that was killing him. He prayed mostly for guidance in every decision and choice he faced. No Terry, let me correct that that would be second because without a doubt he prayed first in thanksgiving for all his blessings everyday."

"It sounds as if he was an incredible man, a good father and wonderful husband."

"He was every bit of that and more, I miss him very much."

"I can understand why you do."

"I do, more than you can imagine. He would be happy to know I went home and talked to Dad and delivered it all on the platter of truth. I now can understand why he said I must go home in truth. As mad as Bernie is and as hard as it is knowing that Dad knows I aborted my baby, Jack was right. We can not change the past, even if it were just yesterday. What we can do is choose for today and tomorrow so our future yesterday is not filled with regret and the haunting pain that sometimes go with it."

"Doris this reconnecting with us, your family may not go very smooth. I can't even guess how anyone else will react when told you are alive, doing well, living in Oregon on a rather large farm. I think most of us believed, if you were still alive, you had a pretty hard existence, a tough life. I don't think any of us even once imagined that you had this kind of life."

"Terry, this is a very normal life. I've been a homemaker, wife and mother doing all the normal things a wife and mother do."

"Doris, just looking around here, by the way how big is this farm?"

"We have a total of thirty seven thousand acres in three areas. We have farm land you see here, grazing land for live stock east of here and timber land up north."

"Do you raise cattle?"

"Yes and other live stock."

"How many head of cattle do you have at any one time?"

"We average fifteen thousand head of livestock at any one time, just what part of that is cattle I don't know."

"Well let me tell you, when the rest of the family hears about you living here in the Northwest on all this land there will be no sympathy and it certainly won't help your reconnecting with everyone. Think it would be easier if you were poor and had it tough."

"Terry, I'm not looking for any sympathy. I walked through Dad's back door last Saturday because it was long past time, and I finally put together the strength and courage to go home and tell Dad I love him and how sorry I am for the horrible choices I made a long time ago. I can't do Dad's part, your part or Bernie's part I can only do what I need to do. If Bernie chooses to remain mad, that is her choice. I really can't say I would do anything different if it was reversed and Bernie was the one who left. I could have left well enough alone but finally well enough was not well enough! None of my family here knows anything about my family in Chicago. They think I'm from Cleveland and lived in foster homes and orphanages, something I just don't talk about. So I chose to make one very big mess for myself when I walked into Dad's kitchen."

"Doris, someday your kids probably would have found out." "Maybe so Terry, I'm glad it's out and I plan to explain everything on Sunday to my family. It won't be easy and I don't even know how they will react, but I am glad to finally explain and let them know they have lots of relatives in Chicago. This is going to be very hard on them too. I know this will hurt them, I just don't know how much."

"What about us, your brothers and sisters? When are you going to talk to all of us?"

"Dad called earlier today and he asked me if he and Joe could explain everything to the family all at one time, sometime this week. He asked if he should tell them about me being pregnant. Of course and the abortion too I told him. I know it is terrible, but it is why I left, the choice I made. He said he would have Joe explain that part. So Terry when you get home, you're going to hear all this again. "Doris, I'm glad I came, maybe I can add something and explain my visit and your side of all this."

"Terry, thank you but don't sell me big. I'm the one who left and I do understand that fact. It is very clear that my long absents from the family and no one knowing where I was or if I was alive or dead is only my fault, all my fault!"

"Doris what do you say we go for a ride and you show me some of your spread?"

"Ha-ha Terry, my spread, very funny, I'd love to. Let's go, I'll take you to the point, that's what we call the spot that overlooks a part of our land, you will see farm land and some used for grazing. It takes about fifteen minutes to get up there."

"Great Doris sounds good to me." "Terry, can you stay and visit for a day, just what is your plan? You told Scott you were leaving tonight."

"I'm flying back to Chicago tonight. I have a flight out of Portland at 6:15; it stops in Denver and arrives in Chicago at1:15 in the morning. I hope to sleep some on the flight."

"Can I take you to dinner, an early dinner at a very nice restaurant and I will then direct you back to the airport and you'll have plenty of time to make your flight?"

"Sure Doris, I would like that very much."

"Good, now let's go sightseeing"

As we drive east from my place I point out to Terry an older white farm house with three out buildings including an old but well kept large red barn. "That's where Scott and Mary Beth live, with their six children. That also is Jacks childhood home, his parents lived there most of their married life. Scott loves this life and pretty much runs the business."

"Scott is the oldest, right?"

"Yes"

"George is my second; he has always been a book worm and teaches at the University of Oregon. He never much liked business or the farm. He teaches literature, and English. My third Margaret Lynn is married to Carl Peterson and they have two girls and own a ranch about thirty five miles southeast of here. Annie my baby is single and lives in Portland and teaches kindergarten. She loves to travel and plans a trip for every summer. She has been all over the world. She's been to Australia and Moscow, every continent. She usually gives at least a few weeks every year doing missionary work somewhere, usually in the south, twice she went to Alaska and worked there."

"Your second son, is he married?"

"Yes, he is married to Carol and they have two children, Claire and Greg."

———•— ·— —•———

"This is a very nice restaurant, 'A Supper Club' and my steak was perfect. Thank you for the very nice treat Doris."

"You're welcome, but I must thank you for your kindness, for coming all this way to Oregon just to meet me and visit with me. I can't describe the happiness I feel meeting you, my brother I didn't even know existed. And Terry, you have been very understanding and accepting. Thank you so much!"

"Doris, this is all so new to me and just so much to take in. Believe me I need time to absorb it all."

"I know.'

'I am glad I met you Doris and heard your story from you. Just getting to know you is helping me understand, I think!"

"Well hearing directly from me didn't make it easy on Bernie."

"Bernie remembers you and missed you as much as Dad and Mom. Give her time."

"I will Terry, I will."

"We are all going to need time."

"I know."

"Doris concentrate on your family right here and I will do my best to take what I found here back with me to all our brothers and sisters." I leaned over to hug Terry and held him never wanting to let go.

Chapter Six

**** *I AM NOT THE ONLY ONE IN THE PICTURE* ****

"Ring"

"Hello"

"Hi Gram"

"Oh, hi Claire, I did not expect to hear your voice. Aunt Mary Beth is going into town and I thought this was her calling for my grocery list; I just needed a few things. How are you doing today Claire?

"I'm alright"

"Good"

"Gram, I can't make it today. I can't help you."

"Are you feeling okay Claire?"

"Yes"

"Are you sure you're okay?"

"I feel sick to my stomach, but I'm okay."

"Claire, is this morning sickness?"

"No, no it's not."

"Something is wrong Claire, I can tell in the sound of your voice."

"Gram, I'll be alright."

"Did you terminate your pregnancy Claire?"

"Yes I did."

"Oh no Claire, why did you do that?"

I move the chair away from the table some and sit down feeling weak and sick to my stomach. Claire continues "Gram, please not now, I don't feel good and I am tired. I didn't sleep well the last couple of nights."

"Yes, I understand that you're not feeling well. I'll take care of everything here."

76

"Thank you Gram, I'm sorry I can't help you out today."

"Get some rest, you need rest. Please call me later and let me know how you're doing. Promise me you will try to sleep and then you will call me later okay?"

"Okay Gram"

"Claire, are your parents aware that I know about this?"

"No, no one knows that you know, no one knows we ever talked. Please don't say anything to my Mom!"

"No, I won't tell her, please call me later."

"I will"

"I love you Claire, I love you. Please take care of yourself".

"I will bye Gram."

I stood up to hang up the telephone and then sat back in the kitchen chair my mind racing with thoughts and at the same time I don't even know what to think. I feel so anxious. I stand and walk over to put water on to boil for tea. I can feel my eyes fill as I say aloud. "God, why did this happen? Why did Claire do this? Why does this have to happen to her?"

"Ring" I grab the phone with a quick snap "Hello".

"Hi Mom, do you have your grocery list ready?"

"Oh Mary Beth I do, yes I do, but I think I will take a ride myself into town. I need to pick up a card and mail it today to a friend who is not feeling well." "Would you like to ride with me?"

"No, not this time, I want to be back quick."

"Suit yourself; I will be at least two hours anyway. Maybe I'll see you in town."

"Thanks Mary Beth"

"Bye Mom, I'll see you tomorrow."

After hanging up the phone I untie my apron and lay it over the back of the chair. In my bedroom I check to see if my check book is in my purse, it is. I grab my jacket and walking back into the kitchen where I see I forget to turn off the tea kettle.

"Ring"

"Oh, God, let that be Claire, please watch over her today, thank You Lord." I pray.

"Ring"

"Hello"

"Hello Doris"

"Yes"

"Hi Doris, this is Bernie."

"Oh, hello Bernie, How are you?"

I pull out the chair again, sit down and set the apron in my lap.

"I'm doing fine, very well. Doris, I talked to Terry last night, he told me much about his visit with you. I want to apologize for the way I spoke to you Sunday. I am sorry."

"I understand Bernie. I can not expect everyone in the family to treat me as if nothing ever happened or like I just woke up from being in a coma for the last 40 years."

"Doris, you were gone all those years, you knew where we were and at any time could dial the phone and talk to us. Mom and Dad wouldn't even sell the house and move because you might come home or call. They never gave up. We even called you 'Hope', because when Annie was about ten, she used you walking in the house someday as an example of Hope for her religion class. Annie never even met you!"

"Bernie, I can't wait to meet Annie and see and visit with all of you."

"I find that hard to understand, after all you did not contact us in forty some years."

"I know, I wish I could change that part of my past. I wish I did call!"

"Why didn't you call? Most of us just accepted that you were dead. I would sometimes wondered if you were out there somewhere being abused or living in poverty or in the street. It was easier to just believe you were dead. If we knew where you were, if we knew your phone number believe me we wouldn't have waited forty some years to call you."

"I'm sorry I ever left home, I'm sorry I did all those terrible things when I was seventeen and then ran away. I can't change the past. I wouldn't change my life, just a few things that happened a long time ago."

"Doris do you know what this did to Mom, do you have any idea?"

"No, I don't, I can't even imagine one of my children running away as I did."

Bernie's voice was filling with anger. I began to massage my forehead and rubbing my eyes as Bernie continued. "The day Mom died, she said she wished you were here. Her nine other children, Paul was already dead, were with her, and she hoped for you. Joe suggested to her that maybe she would be with you soon. Mom paused and said 'No, Doris is not there but Paul is.' she died just a few hours later."

"I figured since you were not in heaven, you were probably in hell and got what you deserved and I found some comfort in that thought."

"It's alright to be angry with me Bernie, I understand…" Bernie cut me off saying.

"Don't you dare tell me it's okay to be angry. You stopped being my big sister a long time ago! Maybe this phone call wasn't a good idea I've got to go."

She hung up. Oh, God, she hung up. She is so mad. I should never have gone home. I should have had a better plan. What do I do now; I was thinking when the door bell rang.

"Hello John, How are you today?"

"I'm well Mrs. Stoner. I have an express overnight letter for you. Please sign here."

"Okay, thank you John."

"Good bye Mrs. Stoner."

"M. Miller, Tinley Park, Illinois"

"Who in the world is M. Miller?"

I opened the cardboard envelope and inside I find a letter addressed to Mrs. Doris Stoner from Maureen Miller. "Could this be Maureen, Maureen Potter? Oh I don't believe it!" I get a knife from the kitchen drawer to open the envelope. The stationary is beautiful a winter scene of snow covered pine trees lining a road up hill to a cabin with little candle lights in the windows and smoke coming from the chimney. "It is from Maureen Potter."

Friday

Dear Doris,

Bernie stopped in at my school this morning on her way to work. She told me about you coming home last weekend. I can't believe I am actually writing you. I can't wait to talk to you and see you again. Bernie told me you lost your husband a few months ago. I am sorry to hear that and please except my condolences. She said you have a family, four children, all raised, of course after all we're sixty-something years old. Bernie said you look great and seemed to have a very full life. I never would guess you would be a farmer and live in Oregon. I can't wait to sit down with you and talk about everything, the fifties, the sixties, the seventies, eighties and now the nineties.

Let me bring you up to speed on some of what has happened in my life. I graduated from CTC and went to work teaching in the Chicago School system. I met Bill Miller in 1956 and we married in 1957. Bill teaches at the community college here. He retired from the Chicago Public Schools three years ago where he taught high school sciences and was principle for 16 years. Currently he teaches Chemistry and Math. We have eight children all grown and on their own. We have nineteen grandchildren and the first set of twins on the way.

We moved into a town-home this past summer and we love it. I miss all the room we had in the big house, although it didn't always seem like there was enough room. I do miss having my own yard.

I went back to work, teaching in 1975 when our youngest started first grade and our oldest was a senior in high school. I love teaching as much as always. Teaching has changed a lot and really is much better. The pay is much better too. I'll never get rich but I truly love teaching.

Doris, I never thought I'd ever see you again. I think of you often and always said a prayer for you. I thank God today that you are well.

I can't wait to find out what your children's names are and how you met your husband. I just can't wait to see you.

Bernie explained that you haven't yet talked to all your brothers and sisters. I know that is more important than talking to me. Just knowing that I will be talking with you soon fills me with joy. When you come back to Chicago to visit please set a few days aside for a visit with me. I would love to have you stay with us. I hope to go to Oregon maybe next summer to see you and meet your family.

I kept in touch with your parents over the years. They never gave up hope of your safe return. Your Dad is doing great on his own. I know your family was concerned when your Mom got sick and died. Your Dad just went on taking care of everything and doing it all very well. He is a good man. I'm sure he's on cloud nine since seeing you. I'll give him a call next week and visit.

I am writing to you from school and I plan to bring this letter to the post office on my way home. Bernie will call me with your address on her lunch hour.

Just a quick mention of a few I keep in touch with. Cathy, Kathy Sue, Donna, Mary and Lynn are all doing well. I am sorry to tell you Terri Murphy Kerr passed away in 1987 from breast cancer. I will wait until after we talk before I call the others to let them know how you are doing.

Doris, please call me anytime and soon, I am really looking forward to our first visit in too many years.

Love you and Happy Your
Well, your friend forever
Maureen Potter Miller
708-555-5555

"What a beautiful letter and nice surprise! And it will be wonderful to talk with Maureen." are my thoughts as I realize it is now ten thirty and I better get to town.

I hold the envelope from Maureen reading her return address and I feel a surge of emotion within me, I am overwhelmingly sad and happy, both at the same time! Sliding the pages out of the envelope, I unfold them and read again. I missed so much, what a crazy thing I did. How can I ever explain all of this to my children? Will Maureen understand? Her letter doesn't sound as if Bernie said anything to her about the abortion. I'm not sure Bernie even knows. Maureen knew I was pregnant but I never told her anything else. What should I say to her now? My eyes are now very heavy with sadness and I wipe my tears with the apron I have in my lap.

I've got to go to town; I'll never get everything done for tomorrow if I don't get going. I would love to talk to Maureen. Should I call her tonight or not? I have all day to think about that. I turn to pick up my jacket I laid over a different chair and slip it on over my sweater. I'm not going to wait; I'm going to call her right now. I already waited too long. I unfold the letter again and dial 708-555-5555.

One ring, two rings.

"Hello"

"Is Maureen in please?" I ask.

"Yes, one minute."

Oh my God, I am so nervous, please help me to say the right things.

"Hello, this is Maureen."

"Hi Maureen, its Doris"

"Oh! Doris! Hello! How are you? _____ Wait let me sit down."

"I'm well. How are you Maureen? Are you alright?"

"I can't believe you called me! You got my letter then?"

"Yes, thank you so much. Maureen, I was surprised and overwhelmingly delighted. I just received you letter and already read it twice, and excited about reading it again, better than that I get to talk with you right now."

"Doris, I've been thinking about you non stop since my visit with Bernie yesterday, I have so many things to ask you and I don't even know where to begin."

"Maureen, please let me start. You're well?"

"Oh yes. My health is great and Bill's also. All my family is doing great. Bill and I have been blessed over and over and over. And you, I know your husband passed away, again I am sorry. I would love to have been able to meet him"

"Thank you, yes I wish Jack met you and everyone back home but that will not be. My health too is good, nothing to complain about except the twenty five extra pounds I carry I don't need."

"I carry spare weight myself. As my Bill says, 'I carry spare weight just incase I looses some.' And your children are they all well?"

"They are all fine, doing great! I too have been more than blessed, and you have eight, Maureen that's a lot of kids!"

"Yes, but it doesn't seem as if it was ever any other way."

"That is a big family, you should be very proud."

"Proud? Yes I am, but 'not a one of us is perfect, just near perfect', another of Bills forever positive sayings."

"He sounds absolutely wonderful."

"He is absolutely wonderful and he would tell you he is! Doris, I can't wait to see you."

"I'll be back in Chicago some time in about a month or so."

You have to come and stay with me a few days please. I'll even take soon time off school, I promise."

"I look forward to seeing you and meeting Mr. Wonderful!" "Oh you'll love him he's great. Doris, tell me about your children and Jack, how did you meet him and end up in Oregon?"

"Oh that is such a long story; I need to go back to when I left home and why."

"Doris we'll start anywhere you want, it's going to take more than one phone call to catch up on the forty five years since we talked."

"You're absolutely right; we won't be able to pay the phone bills! The thought of it is staggering. Maureen, I'm sure you remember I was pregnant when I left."

"Yes that I remember well."

"Well, I didn't run away to have this baby so no one would know. I wanted to come back after being gone two weeks telling my parents and you that I suffered a miscarriage."

"Doris!"

"Wait Maureen, please let me go on."

"Okay, go ahead."

"Well, I knew someone at school who knew where I could get an abortion. My plan was to do just that, then stay away a few weeks, return, with the news of a miscarriage and just go on as if everything was like before. I did, I had an abortion right there, not far from our homes and left town just as I planned. I was headed to New York and planned to stay there for a few weeks, but I couldn't, so I got off the train there and on another headed for Canada. I was trying to hide from myself and what I did. I felt and believed I could never go home and I had to get as far away as possible." "Doris, Bernie told me this."

"She did? You knew this even when you wrote me yesterday?"

"Yes"

"Bernie said your Dad had everyone over on Thursday evening and explained all this to them. I understand Joe and Terry helped to keep the whole thing calm, but most of your family is mad and hurt. Bernie explained they are angry and responded just about the way she did when you saw her last Sunday."

"Bernie told you all this?"

"Yes, she did when she stopped at my school yesterday morning. And when she called at lunch with your address she told me how she was unable to sleep all night, not to mention that she didn't sleep much all week. She was awake thinking and talking to Tom, her husband about everything and why Joe and Terry where the only one's at all excepting of you, your Dad too, of course. Bernie said she needs to talk to you and let you explain and hopefully she will understand and except as Joe and Terry have."

"Bernie, said that?"

"Yes she did, that is what she told me yesterday."

"Maureen, Bernie said she wants to understand, she wants to get through this?"

"Yes"

"And Joe and Terry understand?"

"Yes, well wait a minute Doris, I don't want to miss lead you. Both Joe and Terry have very mixed feelings about all this, the abortion, leaving home, never contacting your Mom and Dad. But they know that they as well as you have to get through all of this."

"Maureen, Bernie called me a little while ago and was very cordial but as we talked, which was only for a few minutes she became upset and said maybe this call wasn't a good idea and that pretty much ended our conversation. Maureen, thank you for telling me this I need to call Bernie back, maybe tomorrow, I'll give her a day or so because I know she is still very upset."

"I think that is a good idea."

"My Dad called here on Tuesday and asked if he and Joe could explain all this to all my brothers and sisters. They felt getting everyone together and explaining with me not there would probably be better. Dad said he or Joe would call me after they all met. I haven't heard from either of them. Maybe they're waiting for things to calm down."

"I don't know Doris. Do you want me to talk to Bernie?"

"No, but thank you, I'll call and talk with her. Maureen, don't tell me you're okay with all of this that I did?"

"No, Doris I'm not, but that was a long time ago and you need to deal with that if you haven't yet, not me."

"Maureen, I have dealt with it a long time ago and many times since. It's not the kind of thing that goes away. We'll talk more when we get together. I want you to know about all of this."

"Doris, whatever you want to tell me is fine. I don't need to know everything or anything."

"I know. Let's talk again this coming week. Tomorrow I am going to explain this entire mess to my children."

"Do they know much about your family?"

"Nothing, absolutely nothing, they are coming for dinner tomorrow and I will try to explain all this."

"Who's coming, just your four children?"

"Yes and their spouses. Three are married, so there will be seven hearing all of this and a lot more, believe me a lot more! Tomorrow is going to be rough to say the least!"

"I'll keep you in my prayers."

Thank you, I will need them. Please pray for my family here and in Chicago?"

"I will"

"Maureen, thank you, I'll call you one evening next week."

"Okay thank you for calling, it is so wonderful to hear your voice again!"

"Thank you for your letter; you will never know what it means to me."

"Okay Doris, bye for now, we will talk next week."

As I hang up the telephone saying to myself "Maureen sounds great! Boy, I can't wait to get all this behind me so I can just get to know everyone again… I will never get this completely behind me and I need to realize that and deal with everything now with my eyes open, head up and moving forward. What I can do is help Claire! I'm not going to go for a card; I'll write her right now and drop a note in her mail box on my way to town."

Dear Claire,

Our telephone conversation earlier today was one I was not at all prepared to have. I anticipated a nice visit with you today while we worked together on the preparations for my dinner tomorrow. The news of your decision to terminate your pregnancy took me by surprise. I know this is a very hard time for you and you are in my thoughts and prayers.

Claire, just after your call I received a letter on beautiful stationary for a long time ago friend. Maureen Potter, now Maureen Miller. I haven't talked with her since 1951. We were best friends through grade school and high school. She just heard yesterday I was living in Oregon and wrote me immediately. She sent the letter overnight mail. I can't describe how wonderful it feels to hear from Maureen. After reading her letter twice I called her. What a joy to talk with her again. It will be months and many conversations before we'll share with each other just a faction of our lives since high school graduation.

Reading Maureen's words sent to me on beautiful stationary made me want to do the same for you. I took from my desk this beautiful stationary you gave me for my birthday a few years ago to write this note to you.

Claire I love you and always will. I want to visit with you soon and tell you all about Maureen. Let's plan a Saturday soon for shopping, lunch and some conversation, just you, me, and the whole day. I will call you next week and you know you can call me anytime, because I love to just talk.

All my love sweet child,
Gram

Chapter Seven

************ *DINNER AND DESSERT* ************

"Welcome, come in Scott, Mary Beth. Why did you knock, the door was unlocked?"

"I wasn't sure if you were hiding any relatives I don't know in here!"

"Oh Scott, stop that, there is not enough room in this house for all our relatives you don't know."

"That's just what I was thinking. Dinner smells wonderful Mom, you're making Italian?"

"Yes I made spaghetti."

"And lemon-meringue pie I hope?"

"Yes Scott and of course I made lemon-meringue pie."

"Mom, just exactly who is Uncle Terry? Scott and I haven't a clue."

"Scott and Mary Beth, I'll explain who Uncle Terry is later. Don't ask because you'll know before you go home today. How about a glass of wine? Scott, would you pour some wine for us? Thank you."

"Everything looks beautiful, the table and the dinner I can't wait."

"Thank you, Mary Beth."

"We're going to eat as soon everyone arrives."

"I expected Annie about an hour ago but I haven't heard from her!"

"They're all here, three cars pulling in the drive right now."

"Scott, did you say everyone is here?"

"Yes Mom, everyone is here."

"Great would you mind pouring wine for all of us and a beer for George and Carl?"

"Hello everyone, come in, please put your jackets in the bedroom."

We all greet each other and Scott invites each to take a glass of wine and he has beer for George and Carl. We are all standing in the kitchen and I move so all can turn as I face them and lift my glass saying "To my family, my children and their spouses who are also my children, I love you all each and every one of you. God has blessed me with a fine family and I am truly grateful. Here's to you each and every one of you!"

"Wow good wine Mom, what kind is this?" asks Annie.

"Chianti, you'll have to look at the bottle to see, I just asked at the liquor store for good Chianti. Annie, I thought you were coming early."

"I was Mom, but I was out late last night, Jerry and I went to his sister Peg's and we played cards until almost three and it was three thirty by the time I got home and in bed. So I slept in and went to the twelve thirty mass."

"Carol would you pour the water from the pot into the coffee maker and hit start, it's all set to go."

"Scott, take the two dishes from the oven and put them on the dining room table, the trivets are on the table already. Everyone sit down I'll bring the pasta right in."

"Mom, everything looks beautiful."

"Thanks Carol"

"It does Mom, why are we eating so soon, we just got here?"

"We are eating first because I have much to tell you and share with you after dinner. First we will eat and enjoy. Does everyone have a salad? Oh, more wine, we will need more wine. I'll grab the bottle on my way." Boys would you like another beer with dinner?"

"Absolutely Mom." Carl answers.

"Make that two" adds George.

"Mom, sit down!"

"I am, let's say our blessing."

All together pray "In the name of the Father, the Son and the Holy Spirit, Amen. Bless us Oh Lord and bless these, our gifts which we are about to receive from thy bounty, through Christ our Lord, Amen. In the name of the Father and the Son and the Holy Spirit, Amen."

"There is plenty of everything, spaghetti, meat balls, garlic bread and I have more of everything in the kitchen!"

"Mom, relax, we will get up if we need more, I mean when we need more."

"Mom, this is one of our favorite meals. I just hope the business you need to discuss is as good!"

"It's not business really George, but it is news, I'll talk later after we eat."

"Mom, how was the wedding Friday night?"

"Margie, it was very nice and so much fun. I dreaded going, the first wedding without your Dad. But freeing a lot of butterflies while I was in Chicago freed me!"

"What? What butterflies did you free? What do you mean?"

"I am talking about the butterflies that should have come out of the cocoons a long time ago. Annie, I will explain all of this shortly. But to answer Margie's question, the wedding was very nice and I had a wonderful time."

"Dinner is delicious!"

"Thank you Mary Beth"

"The big game next Saturday George, are you going to the bash at school again this year?"

"Yes I am, it's always a good time. The alumni throws a great party every year, it is a big fund raiser."

"Well, I know you're all anxious for me to start talking, so let's clear these dishes and pour a cup of coffee and I'll begin. Annie would you please put on another pot of coffee? Thank you. Margie, please grab that tray of cookies and bring them in here on your way back? Thanks Marge."

"Mom, everyone has coffee and we are all sitting down! The floor is yours." "Thank you Scott for that very nice introduction."

"You're welcome. Mom, I never saw you like this before. We rushed through dinner and you're a nervous wreck. Please relax before you have a heart attack!"

"Carl, quiet I'm ready to begin! On Tuesday of this week I was busy around here when I happened to see a man get out of a car and walk up to the house. I opened the door and he asked if I was Doris Stoner. He then introduced himself to me, Terry Hinelick, I'm your youngest brother."

"You have a brother?"

"Yes George, I do, and more than one."

"How many?"

"Please let me continue." "Alright, go ahead"

"Thank you, Scott met my brother when he stopped by that day, I introduced Scott and Terry to each other and simply told Scott I would be explaining all of this on Sunday.

I didn't even know I had a brother Terry; he was born almost two years after I left home. Home was in Chicago not Cleveland. I've never even been to Cleveland except for going through it on a train. When I left home just a few days after my high school graduation my mother was pregnant with my sister Annie. Her baby was due the next fall. Annie is the tenth child of my parents and Terry is the eleventh, and the last. I never met either of them. I have ten brothers and sisters."

"Ten!"

"Yes, ten"

"I am the oldest in my family; there are eight boys and three girls. After me is my brother Jack, then Bernie short for Bernadette, I was closest to Jack and Bernie. Next are twins Frank and Nick, Nicholas, then Joe, Ed and another set of twins Paul and Tom, they were babies when I left. Then Annie was born and a year and a half later Terry. All of my family lives in the Chicago area. My brother Paul one of the second sets of twins is dead. He died in a motorcycle accident in 1969, he was twenty years old. I visited his grave last Sunday, and my mother's they are buried next to each other. My Mom died from cancer May 25th 1992 the same day your father was told he had terminal cancer."

"We have all these aunts and uncles and a grandfather? Is he still living?"

"Yes Marge, you have many aunts and uncles in Chicago and a grandfather who still lives in the house I grew up in. Most of your aunts and uncles are married which gives you even more aunts and uncles. Last weekend I arrived in Chicago and went unannounced to my long ago home. My Dad was shocked to say the least. He told me he and Mom always believed I was alright and would someday return home. He cried, we both cried wishing Mom could have been with us."

"How old is your father and how is his health?" "My Dad, your grandfather is 84 years old and his health is very good. He lives alone and still drives; in the daylight only and he pretty much takes care of himself.

He also has some very nice neighbors who watch out for him. He sees my brothers and sisters often, some he meets regularly. I know he has breakfast one day a week with Frank, Nick and Tom, they took over Dad's business and they get together and talk business, Dad really enjoys it. My Dad was a plumber and he owned a plumbing supply business and was a plumbing contractor. Dad also sees Joe almost every Saturday; they get together for lunch or dinner. My brother Joe is a priest in a Chicago parish. Dad took me to Mass there last Sunday and I heard Mass offered by my brother Father Joseph Heinlick. The last time I saw him he was five years old."

"You have not talked to anyone in your family since you graduated from high school?"

"Yes, that's right."

"That is more that forty years ago!"

"Yes, I know, I left in 1951 almost forty-four years ago. Scott, you haven't said anything, you're very quiet."

"I can't believe what I am hearing Mom! What should I say?"

"Nothing yet, please Scott just listen."

There is silence; all seven are looking at me waiting for me to begin again not daring to speculate on what is to come next. "I visited last week with my Dad and Joe. To my surprise the visit went very well. They both were very loving and understanding, also forgiving. They expressed no judgment of me. They took me over to see my sister Bernie and meet her husband. That did not go well! Bernie first greeted me and asked about you, my family. As I told her about you the built up anger and frustration of forty-four years not knowing if I were okay, alive, dead or what just exploded and she, to put it mildly, gave me a piece of her mind. She was very upset when we left and still was when I spoke with her yesterday on the phone. I was going to stay a few more days and visit with everyone I could but after seeing how Bernie reacted, and I don't blame her, Dad and I decided it would be better for him and Joe to tell everyone and let the news sink in before I knock on any more doors."

"So that's when you came home?"

"Yes Margie."

"Why did you leave home right after high school Mom?"

"I was pregnant at the time Carol."

"What?"

"I was pregnant, three months pregnant."

In high school you got pregnant?

"Yes George, I got pregnant in high school. It wasn't the worst thing in the world, although at that time in my life I sure thought it was. My parents were very upset to say the least, plus my mother was due to have her baby about six weeks before I was due.

They arranged for me to go to a convent in Springfield Illinois until my baby was born. Then the baby would be adopted out. This was the most common thing unwed mothers did at the time, quite different from today."

"Did you go to the convent?"

"No Marge, No I did not. I was planning on going to college that fall, I wanted more than anything to be a teacher. I wanted to teach the little ones first, second, third grade. Had I gone to the convent I would probably be a teacher today."

"Mom, I didn't know you wanted to be a teacher!"

"Yes Annie, I did, I wasn't going to let anything stand in my way either." "Well what happened, what did you do?"

"Believe it or not I prayed for a miscarriage."

"Mom!" a few at the table exclaim.

"I did, I prayed every day."

"Did you have a miscarriage?"

"No, I did not."

"So you gave up the baby? I don't understand?"

"George, I had an abortion."

"What!" again almost all at the table exclaim.

"Yes, I did, I did. I wrote a note to my parents telling them I was going to have the baby on my own, because I wasn't going to a convent. I wrote that I would call them and come home after the baby was born. Oh believe me I had what I thought was a great plan. I was going to have an abortion which I did the day I left home and then take the train to New York for about two weeks. Then I planned to call home and tell my parents I had a miscarriage, go home and everything would be okay. What I never counted on was the way I felt after the abortion. I knew it was wrong, I knew I was killing a baby, my baby but not until then, did I feel the guilt and shame of what I did. The pain was incredible, just horrible, I can't describe how horrible it was. I was physically sick from the abortion but

93

the emotional pain was unbearable. When I arrived in New York I just wanted to die, I knew I could never go back; nothing was ever going to be the same. I purchased a train ticket to Canada, Nova Scotia. You all know the rest of the story."

"Everything you told us after arriving in Nova Scotia is true?"

"Yes Marge. The rest of my life you kids know."

"So you never talked to your parents again or anyone in your family?"

"Not until last weekend Margie when I walked into my father's kitchen."

"There seems to be two separate things you are telling us today. First you are telling us we have numerous relatives we never knew, most or all of them in Chicago. This is interesting, I wish I grew up knowing them, but never the less I am happy to know this now. Second the fact that you had an abortion, this I did not need to know and wish I did not know!"

"Scott, there is a reason I was away from my family all these years and having an abortion is the reason. The reason is not that I was pregnant, it's that I aborted my baby!"

"I really did not need to know that information Mom. Why did you ever tell us this?"

"Scott, I went home. It was time for me to tell the truth." "I thought this was your home!"

"You're right this is my home Scott. This is my home and will always be my home. I have an entire different life I left over forty-four years ago. I had to go back, it is time for me to clear all of this and be honest with everyone."

"What did Daddy know about all of this?

"Everything Annie, he knew everything."

"He knew your family?"

"No, he never met them, but I told him about them. He knew about all of this before we ever dated, I told him when we were friends at the café back in England."

"What did Daddy say?"

"He just listened. Mostly he listened. He told me that my messed up life was my doing and only my doing but mostly he just listened. I know he prayed for me. He believed in prayer and prayed even back then in his twenties when most of us are not praying much. He invited me to go to

Mass with him on some Sundays and to Confession. I first went to Mass with Dad on Easter Sunday and about six or so times before he went state side. It wasn't until I came back to the states that I went to Confession, it was a while before I was able to go to Confession."

"Before your father and I decided to marry we talked about the abortion and he encouraged me to talk to a priest about all of this and of course go to confession. I got in touch with a Franciscan Priest who truly helped me through this. We talked and he advised me to call the baby's father and explain that I was pregnant by him three years ago and I aborted the baby. I replied he never knew about the pregnancy and I asked just what would the point be? Father reminded me that the child I aborted was not only mine but just as much his, and I should have told him than. And it was absolutely necessary to tell him now. Father told me to pray, I remember his words 'Pray, pray hard and tell him as soon as possible.' I asked this priest what I should say to him. He did not know but suggested I remind him of our relationship and explain what transpired from then. I hated the very thought of contacting this guy. He was very nice when I knew him but the only thing I knew about him now was where he went to college. He would be a junior at this time. So I contacted the school he was planning on attending and I explained I was an old friend of his from high school and was trying to locate him. I never expected to be told that he had died in an auto accident about four months earlier. I couldn't believe what I heard. I thought about all of this for months and I realized I kept from him the fact that he did father a child. Maybe had I told him his entire life would have gone another direction, I don't know. This was when I again realized my action three years earlier were purely selfish. The decision I made was only for me and no one else mattered. My baby didn't matter! I simply convinced myself my baby was better off never to breath spring air or smell lilacs, taste ice cream, hear church bells or touch the fleece while hugging a young lamb. My parents didn't matter; after all they did not understand me at all! I never considered my brothers and sisters and most importantly I refused to tell the baby's father, that he was father. My priest friend called me about two months later and we got together. He wanted to see if I ever got in touch with the father of my baby. When I explained the phone call to the college Father just about fell out of his chair. I explained to him how I felt afterwards and my conversation with him that day set in motion a reconciliation process for me that took years to work through. Father then said so softly and peacefully, 'Your baby and his father are together, for eternity.' As I thought about that I felt embarrassed for never telling him about his child. I felt like I got caught. I also felt anger toward him because he was with our child and I was not. He got to know our child and I did not. I actually began to blame him for dying because he had in death what I chose to terminate and eliminate from my life. The realization of what I did three years earlier became clearer than ever. I chose to end a life, a life created by God, entrusted to me and a young man, whom I never told. And now he is dead! At the same visit with Father I explained my relationship with Philip, Scott's father. I was very angry with Philip and Father listened as I explained what had happened, how Philip left and took off for Paris to study. I explained how Philip just left and never looked back. We were married, I was pregnant and none of this made any difference to him. He filed for divorce before he left London and then just left. A few months later I called him and told him his child was born and he had a son, I named him Scott. 'That's fine' was just about all he had to say. He left me and his son in London and never contacted us. My next contact with him was months later about going back to America and taking Scott, he did not care. I concluded by saying to Father. 'I can't believe Philip just left, never contacted us and didn't even want to see his own son.' Father asked me 'How is this any different than what you did to your first child and your family?' It really was not different at all. Today in the 90s many people would say what I did was not at all what Philip did. He abandoned his child and at least I did not bring a child into this world without a mother and father to take care of him. Well the fact of the matter is a young man and I did bring a child into this world. A child I decided did not deserve life! Father suggested that I write Philip and let him know that I am getting married and that Scott is doing fine. He told me to ask Philip to keep in touch with Scott. Well I thought a lot about this and I did write Philip after Jack and I married. I sent him a photo of Scott and our address. But never did anything ever come in return. When Scott was about thirteen he tried contacting his father, remember Scott?. He sent letters to people named Philip Masters in both France and England. He got no positive responses and just let it go. And when he was thirty he received a call from Philip's wife. She explained that Philip had died after a battle with cancer. She told Scott that Philip kept his baby picture under the glass on top of the dresser and it is still there. Scott found out that he had a sister and brother living in London and that is where his father is now buried. It wasn't until after this that I was ready to forgive Philip for abandoning us. I began to pray because I didn't know how to forgive him. I thought about Father, the priest who helped me and how he helped me. I remembered that he said "pray, pray hard". I did and it wasn't long before I was able to let everything go concerning Philip. You would think I had nothing left for Philip after thirty years, but there was still anger. Just a few months or so after this I was explaining to Jack how much better I felt toward Philip and the fact that he never contacted Scott. Jack hoped that Scott would feel some peace soon concerning his father. It was then that your Dad, Jack asked me about the abortion and was I able to put the guilt of that behind me. I remembered something else Father told me way back then he said until I understand and forgive what Philip did I probably wouldn't accept the forgiveness I sought for what I had done. I prayed hard again for forgiveness and it was then that I finally felt forgiveness. I felt forgiveness like I never felt before. I cried scores of times over those years when I thought about aborting my child but this was the first time I felt the warmth of God's love in my tears. I knew I would finally be alright."

"Did you forgive yourself?"

"Did I forgive myself? No, I can't forgive myself. I do accept what I did and I have asked God for forgiveness....I have received and accepted His forgiveness."

"How do you know God has forgiven you?" "Back many years ago I went to confession truly sorry for what I had done, I was given absolution and I accepted absolution knowing I would never repeat my sin again. It was during the time when Dad and I were planning our wedding and I found out that the father of my aborted baby had died. Realizing my baby was dead and the father, he never even knew he was a father, that moment I cried like never before. I never told him he was a father and now he and our child were together, I was left alone. I had your father and Scott but I never felt so alone, so left out. It took time to deal with this. With the help of your Dad and the priest I spoke with I worked through it all as best I could. It is that promise of forgiveness that I still hold on to today. It was after this that Jack again wanted me to get in touch with my parents and siblings. He always encouraged me to contact them but he felt now that I dealt with everything else it was time to mend things with my family. I remember thinking how I didn't deal with other situations until after people died and at that point some things have to be left unsaid. Was I willing to let that happen again? Well I guess I was because I never contacted anyone from my family.

Then just recently a few weeks ago I met a young mother to be, unwed, in high school and ready to abort her child. She was unhappy about the pregnancy. I visited with her in Portland one day while I was there shopping. When I saw her and began talking to her it was like looking in a mirror. I very quickly asked her if she was pregnant. She denied it and we continued to visit. It wasn't long before she explained things to me, not at all much different from what I experienced. She did not tell the baby's father, she did tell her mother, but her Dad didn't know. She told me she was too young to be a mother and had other things to do at this time in her life. Yes she decided with the support of her Mom to have an abortion. We talked for some time about all of this and I explained how I felt about what she was doing. I told her the baby's father needed to know. Also her Dad should be told and somewhere she could find the strength to carry her baby to term and give to a loving adoptive family. I explained how today she could be involved in picking the family. We talked for a few hours and she agreed to rethink her options. I made sure she had my phone number and asked her to call me, keep in touch and I would help her in what ever way I could. It was this chance conversation with this young lady that caused me to again visit my youth, my mistakes and my choices and the consequences of them. I was awake all night thinking about all of this and I wished Jack was there to help me and comfort me. I refused everyone's help 44 years ago and did it my way, now I had to undo, no I can't undo what is done, but patch, mend the wounds and bruises I caused in my parents, brothers and sisters, other relatives, my friends and you my family. It was 4:15 AM when I got out of bed and called information in Chicago and asked for the number of Martin Hinelick and I also wanted to confirm the exact street address. I had written down the address and phone number. I checked periodically over the years but it had been quite a while since I last checked. My next call was United Airlines and I made reservations for a trip to Chicago, my home town, for the next Saturday. I know I always told you I lived in Cleveland, well I didn't. I lived in Chicago, Illinois."

"George and I knew you did live in Chicago not Cleveland."

"How did you know that?"

"Mom, you talked about Marshall Fields and Carson Parie Scott, that's where I always thought my name came from. You talked about State Street. Well when we went to Chicago for the Live Stock Show at the Chicago Stock Yards we realized it was Chicago you talked about, not Cleveland."

"That was when you went with Dad?"

"Yes, I was about fourteen at the time."

"What did Dad say?"

"Cleveland probably had the same stores and every town has a State Street."

"He was probably right Scott, let me continue."

"Go ahead Mom."

"Where was I?"

"You took a flight to Chicago a week ago yesterday."

"That's right Annie. I took a cab from the airport, when I arrived at the house there was a young neighbor just leaving who finished shoveling snow. Our house is on a corner lot in the city and while our house looked very much unchanged, the neighborhood was nothing at all as I remembered. My neighborhood is now inner city. My Dad was standing at the back door as I was getting out of the cab and when I said, "Dad?" with a question mark, he answered "Doris?" also with a question mark. Now let me tell you now about the reunion with my Dad..."

"So you only saw your Dad, Joe and your sister Bernie?"

"No, George I also met Terry this week when he came to visit me."

"Oh yeah, that's right. Now how did he find out all of this?"

"Well, let me see. Joe talked with him about all of this late Sunday night. Terry told me he and Joe are very close and they talk at least four of five times a week. Anyway Joe explained to Terry how I dropped in on Dad and then talked about the day we had together. When Terry wanted to meet me on Monday he called Joe to set it up and Joe explained how I had left to go back to Oregon and that Dad would be explaining this to everyone during the week. Terry then told me that he asked Joe where I lived in Oregon and without saying anything to Joe or Dad he flew here the next day to meet me. And we had what turned out to be a very nice visit. Well that pretty much covers what I wanted to explain to everyone. Do you have any questions about this? What else can I tell you? Pie, maybe we should have a piece of pie."

"No thank you Mom, this is already too much for me to digest. It is way more than I can even think about!" "Scott, is there something you don't understand? You sound upset!"

Actually Mom I don't understand much of any of this! I think I need to head home and let all this just sink in. Mary, are you ready?"

"Sure Scott, okay."

"You know Mom; I'm going to go too."

"Okay Annie, please be careful going home."

I watch through the window as they walk to their cars, Scott walks ahead and gets into his car while Mary Beth and Annie talk briefly, hug and walk toward their cars. On my way back into the dining room I see George, Carol, Carl and Marge all putting on their jackets.

"I think we better get going Mom, unless you want help cleaning up?"

"No, no Margie, I'll take care of this no trouble. Drive safely home."

"We will Mom."

"Good bye Carol, George, I love you."

"Bye Mom"

Margie, we'll talk, I'll call all of you during the week. Love you all, good bye."

Standing on the porch I watch both cars pull out, turning right onto the road. "What a mess I made of everything." I say out loud. I don't know if they will ever be the same. One thing is for sure, I'm truly not the mother they thought I was. And that is very sad! I wonder why they had so little to say and asked so few questions. Maybe I just can't comprehend how this must sound coming from their mother. I might as well clean the dishes. I can't wait until I am done so I can sit down and put my feet up.

It's six thirty in the morning and I'm thinking about calling my father in Chicago. Even though it's two hours later there it is still only eight thirty in Chicago and I think it is still too early to call. I'll try in thirty minutes or so. I'm thinking about how tired I am and the restless night I had when there is a light knock on the door and it opens and in comes Mary Beth.

"Mary Beth, what are you doing here so early, it's only six thirty?"

"Hi Mom, I just thought I would stop by to visit for a while."

"I'm glad you did; let me get you a cup of coffee. Mary Beth, I have to tell you I didn't sleep much last night. I think yesterday was just too much for all of you!"

"I couldn't sleep either Mom. I was up all night thinking about the lemon meringue pie you never cut yesterday. Do you think it would be alright to have a piece at six thirty in the morning?"

Without answering I walked over and we put our arms around each other. We hug silently and then I hear a slight whisper "I love you Mom. We all love you."

"Thank you Mary, thank you."

The End

Mirror Image

Every life experiences bumps, bruises, struggles, conflicts, difficulties and more, these are not forever we make the difference. Often as we journey through life hurts rise both ways. Forgiveness can be confusing and difficult and we sometimes choose to walk right passed it when we need to forgive and even more often when we need forgiveness.

It is easy to see when someone needs forgiveness. Not so easy for us when we need forgiveness, when we justify "There is no forgiveness needed here." or "There is nothing wrong with what I did, I am tired of feeling guilty." Our rest comes in forgiveness, forgiving others and realizing we need forgiveness ourself. "I want to want forgiveness" or "I want to want to forgive" may be a place to start.

Prayer will take you passed that first "want". Prayer is where we start, a "I want to want to prayer" is a start. Get started.

CPSIA information can be obtained
at www.ICGtesting.com
Printed in the USA
LVHW102121070123
736701LV00004B/97